Nora Roberts is the *New York Times* bestselling author of more than one hundred and ninety novels. A born storyteller, she creates a blend of warmth, humour and poignancy that speaks directly to her readers and has earned her almost every award for excellence in her field. The youngest of five children, Nora Roberts lives in western Maryland. She has two sons.

Visit her website at www.noraroberts.com.

Nora Roberts

The Return of
Rafe MacKade

MILLS & BOON

Mills & Boon, an imprint of Harlequin (UK) Limited,
Eton House, 18-24 Paradise Road, Richmond, Surrey TW9 1SR

© Nora Roberts 1995

ISBN: 978 0 263 90454 3

029-0213

Harlequin (UK) policy is to use papers that are natural, renewable and recyclable products and made from wood grown in sustainable forests. The logging and manufacturing processes conform to the legal environmental regulations of the country of origin.

Printed and bound by
CPI Group (UK) Ltd, Croydon, CR0 4YY

To bad boys everywhere

Prologue

The MacKade brothers were looking for trouble. They usually were. In the small town of Antietam, Maryland, it wasn't always easy to find, but then, looking was half the fun.

When they piled into Jared's secondhand Chevy, they'd squabbled over who would take the wheel. It was Jared's car, and he was the eldest, but that didn't carry much weight with his three brothers.

Rafe had wanted to drive. He'd had a need for speed, a thirst to zip along those dark, winding roads, with his foot hard on the gas and his foul and reckless mood chasing behind him. He thought perhaps he could outdistance it, or perhaps meet it head-on. If he met it, bloodied it, conquered it, he knew he would just keep driving until he was somewhere else.

Anywhere else.

They had buried their mother two weeks ago.

Perhaps because his dangerous mood showed so clearly in Rafe's jade eyes and in the cold set of his mouth, he'd been outvoted. In the end, Devin had taken the wheel, with Jared riding shotgun. Rafe brooded in the back seat with his youngest brother, Shane, beside him.

They were a rough and dangerous group, the MacKade boys. All of them tall and rangy as wild stallions, with fists ready and often too eager to find a target. Their eyes, MacKade eyes, all varying shades of green, could carve a man into pieces at ten paces. When the dark mood was on them, a wise man stayed back eleven or more.

They settled on pool and beer, though Shane complained, as he was still shy of twenty-one and wouldn't be served in Duff's Tavern.

Still, the dim, smoke-choked bar suited them. The slam and crack of the balls had just enough of a violent edge, the gaze of the scrawny-shouldered Duff Dempsey was just uneasy enough. The wariness in the eyes of the other customers, gossiping over their beers, was just flattering enough.

Nobody doubted the MacKade boys were out for trouble. In the end, they found what they were looking for.

While a cigarette dangled from the corner of his mouth, Rafe squinted against the smoke and eyed his shot. He hadn't bothered to shave in a couple of days, and the rough stubble mirrored his mood. With a solid smack, a follow-through smooth as silk, he banked the cue ball, kissed it off the seven and made his pocket.

"Good thing you're lucky at something." At the bar, Joe Dolin tipped back his beer. He was, as usual after sundown, mostly drunk, and mean with it. He'd once been the star of the high school football team, had competed with the MacKades for the favors of pretty young girls. Now, at barely twenty-one, his face had begun to bloat and his body to sag.

The black eye he'd given his young wife before leaving the house hadn't really satisfied him.

Rafe chalked his cue and barely spared Joe a glance.

"Going to take more than hustling pool, MacKade, to keep that farm going, now that your mama's gone." Dangling his bottle from two fingers, Joe grinned.

"Heard you're going to have to start selling off for back taxes."

"Heard wrong." Coolly Rafe circled the table to calculate his next shot.

"Oh, I heard right. You MacKades've always been fools, and liars."

Before Shane could leap forward, Rafe shot out his cue to block the way. "He's talking to me," he said quietly. He held his brother's gaze another moment before he turned. "Isn't that right, Joe? You're talking to me?"

"I'm talking to any of you." As he lifted his beer again, Joe's gaze skimmed over the four of them. At twenty, Shane was tough from farm work, but still more boy than man. Then Devin, whose cool, thoughtful gaze revealed little. Over Jared, who was leaning negligently against the jukebox, waiting for the next move.

He looked back at Rafe. There was temper, hot and ready. Recklessness worn like a second skin. "But you'll do. Always figured you for the biggest loser of the lot, Rafe."

"That so?" Rafe crushed out his cigarette, lifted his own beer. He drank as they completed the ritual before battle, and customers shifted in their chairs to watch. "How're things going at the factory, Joe?"

"Least I get a paycheck," Joe shot back. "I got money in my pocket. Ain't nobody going to take my house from over me."

"Not as long as your wife keeps putting in twelve-hour shifts working tables to pay the rent."

"Shut your mouth about my wife. I earn the money in my house. I don't need no woman paying my way, like your mama had to do for your old man. Went through her inheritance like it was water, then up and died on her."

"Yeah, he died on her." Anger and guilt and grief welled up inside him. "But he never laid a hand on her. She never had to come into town hiding behind scarves and dark glasses, and saying how she took a fall. Only thing your mother ever fell over, Joe, was your father's fist."

Joe slammed his beer onto the bar, shattering the glass. "That's a lie. I'm going to ram that lie down your throat."

"Try it."

"He's drunk, Rafe," Jared murmured.

Those lethal green eyes sliced toward his brother. "So?"

"So there isn't much point in breaking his face

when he's drunk." Jared moved a shoulder. "He's not worth it."

But Rafe didn't need a point. He just needed action. He lifted his cue, studied it, then laid it across the table. "You want to take me on, Joe?"

"Don't you start in here." Though he knew it was already too late, Duff jerked a thumb toward the wall phone. "You make any trouble in here, I'm calling the sheriff, and the lot of you can cool off in jail."

"Keep your damn hand off the phone," Rafe warned him. His eyes were hard enough to have the bartender backing off. "Outside," he said simply.

"You and me." Curling his fists, Joe stared at the MacKades. "I ain't having your brothers jumping in on me while I whip your butt."

"I don't need any help with you." To prove it, the moment they cleared the door Rafe pivoted to avoid Joe's swing, rammed his fist into Joe's face and felt the first satisfying spill of blood.

He couldn't even have said why he was fighting. Joe meant less to him than the dust in the street. But it felt good. Even when Joe got past his guard and connected, it felt good. Fists and blood were the only clear solution. When he felt the satisfying crack of knuckles against bone, he could forget everything else.

Devin winced, then tucked his hands philosophically in his pockets when blood spurted from his brother's mouth. "I give it five minutes."

"Hell, Rafe'll take him down in three." Grinning, Shane watched the grunting opponents wrestle to the ground.

"Ten bucks."

"You're on. Come on, Rafe!" Shane shouted. "Whip his sorry butt!"

It took three minutes, plus thirty nasty seconds with Rafe straddling Joe and methodically pumping a fist into his face. Since Joe's eyes had rolled up white and his arms were limp at his sides, Jared stepped forward to drag his brother away.

"He's finished." To decide the matter, Jared rammed Rafe up against the brick wall of the bar. "He's finished," he repeated. "Let it go."

The vicious rage drained slowly, fading from Rafe's eyes, uncurling his fists. Emptying him. "Let go, Jare. I'm not going to hit him again."

Rafe looked to where Joe lay moaning, half-unconscious. Over his battered body, Devin counted out bills for Shane. "I should have factored in how drunk he was," Devin commented. "If he'd been sober, it would've taken Rafe the five."

"Rafe would never waste five full minutes on a punk like that."

Jared shook his head. The arm that was restraining Rafe slipped companionably around Rafe's shoulders. "Want another beer?"

"No." He glanced toward the window of the bar, where most of the patrons had gathered to watch. Absently he swiped blood from his face. "Somebody better pick him up and haul him home," he called out. "Let's get out of here."

When he settled in the car again, the aches and bruises began to make themselves known. With half an ear, he listened to Shane's enthusiastic play-by-play of the bout and used Devin's bandanna to mop more blood from his mouth.

He was going nowhere, he thought. Doing nothing. Being nothing. The only difference between him and Joe Dolin was that Joe was a drunk on top of it.

He hated the damn farm, the damn town, the damn trap he could feel himself sinking into with every day that passed.

Jared had his books and studies, Devin his odd and ponderous thoughts, Shane the land that seemed to delight him.

He had nothing.

On the edge of town, where the land began to climb and the trees to thicken, he saw a house. The old Barlow place. Dark, deserted and haunted, so it was said. It stood alone, unwanted, with a reputation that caused most of the townspeople to ignore it or eye it warily.

Just as they did Rafe MacKade.

"Pull over."

"Hell, Rafe, you going to be sick?" Not concerned so much as apprehensive, Shane gripped his own door handle.

"No. Pull over, damn it, Jared."

The minute the car stopped, Rafe was out and climbing the rocky slope. Brambles thick with thorns and summer growth tore at his jeans. He didn't need to look behind or hear the curses and mutters to know that his brothers were following him.

He stood, looking up at three stories of local stone. Mined, he supposed, from the quarry a few miles out of town. Some of the windows were broken and boarded, and the double porches sagged like an old woman's back. What had once been a lawn was over-grown with wild blackberries, thistles and witchgrass. A dead oak rose from it, gnarled and leafless.

But as the moon wheeled overhead and the breeze sang chants through the trees and tall grass, there was something compelling about the place. The way it stood two hundred years after its foundation had been laid. The way it continued to stand against time, weather and neglect. And most of all, he thought, the way it stood against the distrust and gossip of the town it overlooked.

"Going to look for ghosts, Rafe?" Shane stood beside him, eyes gleaming against the dark.

"Maybe."

"Remember when we spent the night there, on a dare?" Absently Devin plucked a blade of grass, rolled it between his fingers. "Ten years ago, I guess it was. Jared snuck upstairs and started creaking doors. Shane wet his pants."

"Hell I did."

"Hell you didn't."

This incited the predictable shoving match, which the older brothers ignored.

"When are you leaving?" Jared said quietly. He'd

known it, saw it now in the way Rafe looked at the house, into it, beyond it.

"Tonight. I've got to get away from here, Jare. Do something away from here. If I don't, I'm going to be like Dolin. Maybe worse. Mom's gone. She doesn't need me anymore. Hell, she never needed anybody."

"Got any idea where you're going?"

"No. South, maybe. To start." He couldn't take his eyes off the house. He would have sworn it was watching him, judging him. Waiting. "I'll send money when I can."

Though he felt as though someone were wrenching off one of his limbs, Jared merely shrugged. "We'll get by."

"You have to finish law school. Mom wanted that." Rafe glanced behind, to where the shoving match had progressed to wrestling in the weeds. "They'll handle themselves okay once they figure out what they want."

"Shane knows what he wants. The farm."

"Yeah." With a thin smile, Rafe took out a cigarette. "Go figure. Sell off some of the land, if you have to, but don't let them take it. We have to keep what's ours. Before it's over, this town's going to remember the MacKades meant something."

Rafe's smile widened. For the first time in weeks, the gnawing ache inside him eased. His brothers were sitting on the ground, covered with dirt and scratches and laughing like loons.

He was going to remember them that way, he promised himself, just that way. The MacKades, holding together on rocky ground no one wanted.

Chapter 1

The bad boy was back. The town of Antietam was buzzing over it, passing fact, rumor and innuendo from one to another, the way the guests at a boardinghouse passed bowls of steaming stew.

It was a rich broth, spiced with scandal, sex and secrets. Rafe MacKade had come back after ten years.

Some said there would be trouble. Bound to be. Trouble hung around Rafe MacKade like a bell around a bull's neck. Wasn't it Rafe MacKade who'd decked the high school principal one spring morning and gotten himself expelled? Wasn't it Rafe MacKade who'd wrecked his dead daddy's Ford pickup before he was old enough to drive?

And surely it was Rafe MacKade who'd tossed a table—and that fool Manny Johnson—through the plate-glass window of Duff's Tavern one hot summer night.

Now he'd come back, a-riding into town in some fancy sports car and parking, bold as you please, right in front of the sheriff's office.

Of course, his brother Devin was sheriff now, had been for five years last November. But there'd been a time—and most remembered—when Rafe MacKade spent more than a night or two in one of the two cells in the back.

Oh, he was as handsome as ever—so the women said. With those devil's good looks the MacKades were gifted—or cursed—with. If a female had breath in her body, she'd look twice, maybe even sigh over that long, wiry build, that loose-legged stride that seemed to dare anyone to get in the way.

Then there was that thick black hair, those eyes, as green and hard as the ones in that little Chinese statue in the window of the Past Times antique store. They did nothing to soften that tough, sharp-jawed face, with that little scar along the left eye. God knew where he'd gotten that.

But when he smiled, when he curved that beautiful mouth up and that little dimple winked at the corner, a woman's heart was bound to flutter. That sentiment came directly from Sharilyn Fenniman who'd taken that smile, and his twenty dollars for gas, at the Gas and Go, just outside of town.

Before Rafe had his car in gear again, Sharilyn had been burning up the phone wires to announce the return.

"So Sharilyn called her mama, and Mrs. Metz got right on her horse and told Mrs. Hawbaker down at the general store that Rafe maybe plans to stay."

As she spoke, Cassandra Dolin topped off Regan's coffee. The way snow was spitting out of the January sky and clogging streets and sidewalks, there was little business at Ed's Café that afternoon. Slowly Cassie straightened her back and tried to ignore the ache in her hip where it had struck the floor after Joe knocked her down.

"Why shouldn't he?" Smiling, Regan Bishop loitered over her mulligan stew and coffee. "He was born here, wasn't he?"

Even after three years as a resident and shopkeeper of Antietam, Regan still didn't understand the town's fascination with comings and goings. It appealed to and amused her, but she didn't understand it.

"Well, yeah, but he's been gone so long. Only came back for a day or so at a time, once or twice in ten whole years." Cassie looked out the window, where the snow fell thin and constant. And wondered where he had gone, what he had seen, what he had done. Oh, she wondered what there was out there.

"You look tired, Cassie," Regan murmured.

"Hmm? No, just daydreaming. This keeps up, they're going to call school early. I told the kids to come straight here if they did, but..."

"Then that's what they'll do. They're great kids."

"They are." When she smiled, some of the weariness lifted from her eyes.

"Why don't you get a cup? Have some coffee with me?" A scan of the café showed Regan there was a customer in a back booth, dozing over his coffee, a couple at the counter chatting over the stew special. "You're not exactly overrun with business." Seeing Cassie hesitate, Regan pulled out her trump. "You could fill me in on this Rafe character."

"Well." Cassie nibbled on her lip. "Ed, I'm going to take a break, okay?"

At the call, a bony woman with a frizzed ball of red hair stuck her head out of the kitchen. Sparkling-framed glasses rested on her scrawny chest, above her bib apron. "You go ahead, honey." Her low voice rasped from two packs of cigarettes a day. Her face was carefully painted from red lips to red eyebrows, and glowed from the heat of the stove. "Hey there, Regan. You're fifteen minutes over your lunch hour."

"I closed at noon," Regan told her, well aware that her clocklike schedule amused Edwina Crump. "People aren't looking for antiques in this kind of weather."

"It's been a hard winter." Cassie brought a cup to the table and poured coffee for herself. "We're not even through January, and the kids are already getting tired of sledding and making snowmen." She sighed, careful not to wince when the bruise on her hip ached when she sat. She was twenty-seven, a year younger than Regan. She felt ancient.

After three years of friendship, Regan recognized the signs. "Are things bad, Cassie?" Keeping her voice low, she laid a hand over Cassie's. "Did he hurt you again?"

"I'm fine." But Cassie kept her eyes on her cup.

Guilt, humiliation, fear, stung as much as a backhand slap. "I don't want to talk about Joe."

"Did you read the pamphlets I got you, about spousal abuse, the women's shelter in Hagerstown?"

"I looked at them. Regan, I have two children. I have to think of them first."

"But—"

"Please." Cassie lifted her gaze. "I don't want to talk about it."

"All right." Struggling to hold back the impatience, Regan squeezed her hand. "Tell me about bad boy MacKade."

"Rafe." Cassie's face cleared. "I always had a soft spot for him. All of them. There wasn't a girl in town who didn't moon a few nights over the MacKade brothers."

"I like Devin." Regan sipped at her coffee. "He seems solid, a little mysterious at times, but dependable."

"You can count on Devin," Cassie agreed. "Nobody thought any of them would turn out, but Devin makes a fine sheriff. He's fair. Jared has that fancy law practice in the city. And Shane, well, he's rough around the edges, but he works that farm like two mules. When they were younger and they came barreling into town, mothers locked up their daughters, and men kept their backs to the wall."

"Real upstanding citizens, huh?"

"They were young, and always seemed angry at something. Rafe most of all. The night he left town, Rafe and Joe got into it over something. Rafe broke Joe's nose and knocked out a couple of his teeth."

"Really?" Regan decided she might like this Rafe after all.

"He was always looking for a fight, Rafe was. Their father died when they were kids. I'd have been about ten," she mused. "Then their mama passed on, right before Rafe left town. She'd been sick nearly a year. That's how things at the farm got so bad around then. Most people thought the MacKades would have to sell out, but they held on."

"Well, three of them did."

"Mmm..." Cassie savored the coffee. It was so rare to have a moment just to sit. "They were barely more than boys. Jared would have been right about twenty-three, and Rafe's just ten months behind him. Devin's about four years older than me, and Shane's a year behind him."

"Sounds like Mrs. MacKade was a busy woman."

"She was wonderful. Strong. She held everything together, no matter how bad it got. I always admired her."

"Sometimes you need to be strong to let things go," Regan murmured. She shook her head. She'd promised herself she wouldn't push. "So, what do you think he's come back for?"

"I don't know. They say he's rich now. Made a pile buying land and houses and selling them again. He's supposed to have a company and everything. MacKade. That's what he calls it. Just MacKade. My mother always said he'd end up dead or in jail, but..."

Her voice trailed off as she looked through the window. "Oh, my," she murmured. "Sharilyn was right."

"Hmm?"

"He looks better than ever."

Curious, Regan turned her head just as the door jingled open. As black sheep went, she was forced to admit, this one was a prime specimen.

He shook snow from thick hair the color of coal dust and shrugged off a black leather bomber jacket that wasn't meant for East Coast winters. Regan thought he had a warrior's face—the little scar, the unshaven chin, the slightly crooked nose that kept that mouth-watering face from being too pretty.

His body looked hard as granite, and his eyes, sharp green, were no softer.

In worn flannel, torn jeans and scarred boots, he didn't look rich and successful. But he sure looked dangerous.

It amused and pleased Rafe to see Ed's place was so much the same. Those could be the same stools at the counter that he'd warmed his seat on as a child, antici-pating a sundae or a fountain drink. Surely those were the same smells—grease, frying onions, the haze from Ed's constant cigarettes, an undertone of pine cleaner.

He was sure Ed would be back in the kitchen, flip-ping burgers or stirring pots. And sure as hell that was old man Tidas snoring in the back booth while his cof-fee went cold. Just as he'd always done.

His eyes, cool, assessing, skimmed over the pain-fully white counter, with its clear-plastic-topped plates of pies and cakes, over the walls, with their black-and-white photos of Civil War battles, to a booth where two women sat over coffee.

He saw a stranger. An impressive one. Honey brown hair cut in a smooth chin-length swing that framed a face of soft curves and creamy skin. Long lashes over dark and coolly curious blue eyes. And a sassy little mole right at the corner of a full and unsmiling mouth.

Picture-perfect, he thought. Just like something cut out of a glossy magazine.

They studied each other, assessed each other as a man or woman might assess a particularly attractive trinket in a shop window. Then his gaze shifted to land on the fragile little blonde with the haunted eyes and the hesitant smile.

"Son of a bitch." His grin flashed and upped the temperature by twenty degrees. "Little Cassie Connor."

"Rafe. I heard you were back." The sound of her giggle as Rafe plucked her from the booth had Regan's brow lifting. It was rare to hear Cassie laugh so freely.

"Pretty as ever," he said, and kissed her full on the lips. "Tell me you kicked that idiot out and left the path clear for me."

She eased back, always fearful of wagging tongues. "I've got two kids now."

"A boy and a girl. I heard." He tugged the strap of her bib apron, and thought with some concern that she'd lost too much weight. "You're still working here?"

"Yeah. Ed's in the back."

"I'll go see her in a minute." Resting a hand casually on Cassie's shoulder, he looked back at Regan. "Who's your pal?"

"Oh, sorry. This is Regan Bishop. She owns Past Times, an antique and decorating store a couple doors down. Regan, this is Rafe MacKade."

"Of the MacKade brothers." She offered a hand. "Word's already traveled."

"I'm sure it has." He took her hand, held it, as his eyes held hers. "Antiques? That's a coincidence. I'm in the market."

"Are you?" She'd risk her dignity if she tugged her hand from his. From the gleam in his eye, she was sure he knew it. "Any particular era?"

"Mid-to-late-1800s—everything from soup to nuts. I've got a three-story house, about twelve hundred square feet to furnish. Think you can handle it?"

It took a lot of willpower for her to keep her jaw from dropping. She did well enough with tourists and townspeople, but a commission like this would easily triple her usual income.

"I'm sure I can."

"You bought a house?" Cassie said interrupting them. "I thought you'd be staying out at the farm."

"For now. The house isn't for living in, not for me. After some remodeling, restoring, I'll be opening it up as a bed-and-breakfast. I bought the old Barlow place."

Stunned, Cassie bobbled the coffeepot she'd fetched. "The Barlow place? But it's—"

"Haunted?" A reckless light glinted in his eyes. "Damn right it is. How about a piece of that pie to go with the coffee, Cassie? I've worked up an appetite."

Regan had left but Rafe had loitered for an hour, entertained when Cassie's kids burst in out of the snow. He watched her fuss over them, scold the boy for forgetting to put on his gloves, listened to the big-eyed little girl solemnly relate the adventures of the day.

There was something sad, and somehow soothing, about watching the girl he remembered settling her two children at a booth with crayons and books.

A lot had stayed the same over a decade. But a lot had changed. He was well aware that news of his arrival was even now singing over telephone wires. It pleased him. He wanted the town to know he was back—and not with his tail between his legs, as many had predicted.

He had money in his pocket now, and plans for the future.

The Barlow place was the heart of his plans. He didn't subscribe to ghosts, under most circumstances, but the house had certainly haunted him. Now it belonged to him, every old stone and bramble—and whatever else it held. He was going to rebuild it, as he had rebuilt himself.

One day he would stand at the top window and look down on the town. He would prove to everyone—even to Rafe MacKade—that he was somebody.

He tucked a generous tip under his cup, careful to keep the amount just shy of one that would embarrass Cassie. She was too thin, he thought, and her eyes were too guarded. That weary fragility had been thrown into sharp relief when she sat with Regan.

Now there was a woman, he mused, who knew how to handle herself. Steady eyes, stubborn chin, soft hands. She hadn't so much as blinked when he offered her a shot at furnishing an entire inn. Oh, he imagined her insides had jolted, but she hadn't blinked.

As a man who'd earned his keep on the wheel and

deal, he had to admire her for it. Time would tell if she'd hold up to the challenge.

And there was no time like the present.

"That antique place, two doors down?"

"That's right." Cassie kept one eye on her children as she brewed a fresh pot of coffee. "On the left. I don't think she's open, though."

Rafe shrugged into his jacket and grinned. "Oh, I bet she is."

He strolled out, hatless, jacket open, his footsteps muffled by the cushioning snow. As he'd expected, the lights were on inside Past Times. Instead of seeking shelter inside, he studied her window display and found it clever and effective.

A sweep of blue brocade like a pool of shimmering water flowed over varying levels. A bright-eyed porcelain doll sat on a child-size ladder-back rocker, an artful tumble of antique toys at her feet. A snarling jade dragon curled on a pedestal. A glossy mahogany jewelry box stood open, glittery baubles spilling out of its drawers as though a woman's hands had slid through them in search of just the right piece.

Perfume bottles were arranged in pretty sunbursts of color on an enameled shelf.

Put the sparkles up front, he thought with a nod, and rope the customers in.

Sleigh bells hung on the door tinkled musically when he opened it. The air inside was spiced with cinnamon and cloves and apples. And, he realized after a deep breath of it, of Regan Bishop. The subtle and sultry perfume he'd noted in the café just teased the air.

He took his time wandering. Furniture was meticulously arranged for traffic patterns. A settee here, an occasional table there. Lamps, bowls, vases, all doing double duty as display and decoration. A dining room table was gracefully set with china and glassware, candles and flowers, as if guests were expected any moment. An old Victrola stood open beside a cabinet filled with 78s.

There were three rooms, each as polished and organized as the last. Nowhere in her inventory did he notice a single speck of dust. He paused by a kitchen hutch filled with white stoneware dishes and blue-tinted mason jars.

"It's a nice piece," Regan said from behind him.

"We have one like this in the kitchen at the farm." He didn't turn. He'd known she was there. "My mother kept the everyday dishes in it. White ones, like these.

And glasses. Thick ones that didn't break easy. She threw one at me once when I sassed her."

"Did she hit you?"

"No. Would have if she'd meant to." Now he turned and flashed that killer grin. "She had a hell of an arm. What are you doing in the middle of nowhere, Regan Bishop?"

"Selling my wares, Rafe MacKade."

"Your wares aren't half-bad. How much for the dragon in the window?"

"You have excellent taste. It's five-fifty."

"That's steep, Regan." Reaching out, he slipped open the single gold button of her navy blazer.

She found the little gesture oddly intimate, but refused to comment on it. "You get what you pay for."

"If you're smart, you can get more." He tucked his thumbs in the front pockets of his jeans and began to wander again. "How long have you been in town?"

"Three years last summer."

"From?" When she didn't answer, he glanced back, lifted one of those sexy black brows. "Just making conversation, darling. I like to get a handle on the people I'm doing business with."

"We haven't done any business, yet." She tucked her hair behind her ear and smiled. "Darling."

His laugh erupted, quick and charming. Little ripples of response skidded up her spine. He was, she was sure, the man every mother had ever warned her daughter about. As tempting as it was, business was business. And it always came first.

"I think I'm going to like you, Regan." He tilted his head. "You sure are a looker."

"Making conversation again?"

"An observation." With a smile hovering around his mouth, he glanced down at her hands. She wore rings, pretty, glittery stones and twists of gold. "Any of those mean anything that's going to get in my way?"

Her stomach fluttered. Her spine stiffened. "I'd say that depends on which way you're heading."

"Nope," he declared. "You're not married. You'd have tossed that in my face. So." Satisfied, he sat on a red velvet love seat, tossed his arm over the curved back. "Want to sit down?"

"No, thanks. Did you come in to do business, or to talk me into bed?"

"I never talk women into bed." He smiled at her.

No, she thought, he'd just have to flash that smile and crook his finger.

"Business, Regan." Relaxed, he crossed his booted feet. "For now, just business."

"All right. Then I'll offer you some hot cider."

"I'll take it."

She moved through a doorway, into the back. Alone, Rafe brooded for a moment. He hadn't meant to be so obvious, hadn't realized he was quite so attracted. There had been something about the way she stood there, in her tailored blazer and tasteful jewelry, her eyes so cool and amused, her scent just short of hot.

If he'd ever seen a woman who announced a thorny road, it was Regan Bishop. Though he rarely chose the smooth path, he had too much on his plate to take the challenge.

Then she came back in on those long, glamorous legs, that pretty swing of hair half curtaining her face.

What the hell, he thought, he could always make room on his plate.

"Thanks." He took the steaming enameled mug she offered. "I figured on hiring a firm out of D.C. or Baltimore, maybe taking some time to hunt through some shops myself."

"I can acquire anything a firm in D.C. or Baltimore can, and offer a better price." She hoped.

"Maybe. The thing is, I like the idea of keeping the business close to home. We'll see what you can do." He sipped the cider, found it hot and pungent. "What do you know about the Barlow place?"

"It's falling apart. I think it's a crime that nothing's been done to preserve it. This part of the country is usually careful with its historic areas and buildings. But the town ignores that place. If I had the means, I'd have bought it myself."

"And you'd have gotten more than you bargained for. The house is solid as rock. If it wasn't so well built, it'd be rubble by now. But, it needs work..." he mused, and began to picture it all in his head. "Floors to be leveled and sanded and sealed, walls to be plastered or taken down, windows replaced. The roof's a mess."

He brought himself back, shrugged. "That's just time and money. When it's ready, I want to put it back the way it looked in 1862, when the Barlows lived there and watched the Battle of Antietam from their parlor window."

"Did they?" Regan asked with a smile. "I'd have thought they'd have been cowering in the root cellar."

"Not the way I imagine it. The rich and privileged watching the show, maybe annoyed when cannon fire cracked a window or the screams of the dead and dying woke the baby from its nap."

"You're a cynical one. Being rich wouldn't mean you wouldn't feel horror if you had to watch men dying on your front lawn."

"The heart of the battle didn't get quite that close. Anyway, that's what I want—the right colors, trim, wallpaper, furnishings, doodads. The works." He had an urge for a cigarette and banked it. "How do you feel about redoing a haunted house?"

"Interested." She eyed him over the rim of her mug. "Besides, I don't believe in ghosts."

"You will before it's done. I spent the night there once, as a kid, with my brothers."

"Creaking doors, rattling chains?"

"No." He didn't smile now. "Except the ones Jared arranged to scare the guts out of the rest of us. There's a spot on the stairway that'll turn your skin to ice. You can smell smoke near the living room hearth. And you can feel something looking over your shoulder when you walk down the hallways. If it's quiet enough, and you're listening, you can hear sabers clash."

Despite herself, she couldn't quite suppress a shudder. "If you're trying to scare me off the commission, you won't."

"Just laying out the blueprint. I'll want you to take a look at the place, go through the rooms with me. We'll see what kind of ideas you have. Tomorrow afternoon suit you? About two?"

"That'll be fine. I'll need to take measurements."

"Good." He set his mug aside, rose. "Nice doing business with you."

Again she accepted his hand. "Welcome home."

"You're the first one who's said it." Enjoying the irony, he lifted her hand to his lips, watching her. "Then again, you don't know any better. See you tomorrow. And, Regan," he added on his way to the door, "take the dragon out of the window. I want it."

On the way out of town, he pulled his car to the side of the road and stopped. Ignoring the snow and the icy fingers of the wind, he studied the house on the rise of the hill.

Its broken windows and sagging porches revealed nothing, just as Rafe's shadowed eyes revealed nothing. Ghosts, he mused, while snow drifted silently around him. Maybe. But he was beginning to realize that the only ghosts he was trying to put to rest were inside him.

Chapter 2

The beauty of owning your own shop, as far as Regan was concerned, was that you could buy and sell what you chose, your hours were your own to make, and the atmosphere was your own to create.

Still, being the sole proprietor and sole employee of Past Times didn't mean Regan Bishop tolerated any slack. As her own boss, she was tough, often intolerant, and expected the best from her staff. As that staff, she worked hard and rarely complained.

She had exactly what she'd always wanted—a home and business in a small rural town, away from the pressures and headaches of the city where she'd lived the first twenty-five years of her life.

Moving to Antietam and starting her own business had been part of her five-year plan after she graduated from American University. She had degrees in history and business management tucked under her belt, and by the time she donned cap and gown she'd already earned five years experience in antiques.

Working for someone else.

Now she was the boss. Every inch of the shop and the cozy apartment atop it was hers—and the bank's. The MacKade commission was going to go a long way toward making her share a great deal larger.

The minute Rafe left the afternoon before, Regan had locked up and dashed to the library. She'd checked out an armload of books to supplement her own research volumes.

By midnight, when her eyes had threatened to cross, she had read and taken notes on every detail of life as it applied to the Civil War era in Maryland.

She knew every aspect of the Battle of Antietam, from Lee's march to his retreat across the river, from McClellan's waffling to President Lincoln's visit to a farm outside Sharpsburg. She knew the number of dead and wounded, the bloody progress over hill and through cornfield.

It was sad and standard information, and she'd studied it before. Indeed, her fascination with the battle and the quiet area into which it had exploded had influenced her choice of a home.

But this time she'd been able to find bits and pieces on the Barlows—both fact and speculation. The family had lived in the house on the hill for almost a hundred years before that horrible day in September of 1862. Prosperous landowners and businessmen, they had lived like lords. Their balls and dinners had enticed guests from as far as Washington and Virginia.

She knew how they had dressed—the frock coats and lace and the hooped skirts. Silk hats and satin slippers. She knew how they had lived, with servants pouring wine into crystal goblets, their home decorated with hothouse flowers, their furniture glowing with bee's wax polish.

Now, negotiating snowy, windy roads under sparkling sunlight, she could see exactly the colors and fabrics, the furnishings and knickknacks that would have surrounded them.

Chiffoniers of rosewood, she mused. Wedgwood china and horsehair settees. The fine Chippendale chest-on-chest for the master, the graceful cherrywood-and-beveled-glass secretaire for his lady. Brocade portieres and rich Colonial blue for the walls in the parlor.

Rafe MacKade was going to get his money's worth. And, oh, she hoped his pockets were deep.

The narrow, broken lane leading up to the house was deep in snow. No tire tracks or handy plow had marred its pretty, pristine—and very inconvenient—white blanket.

Annoyed that Rafe hadn't taken care of that detail, Regan eased her car onto the shoulder.

Armed with her briefcase, she began the long trudge up.

At least she'd thought to wear boots, she told herself as the snow crept past her ankles. She'd very nearly worn a suit and heels—before she remembered that impressing Rafe MacKade wasn't on her agenda. The gray trousers, tailored blazer and black turtleneck were acceptable business wear for an assignment such as this. And, as she doubted the place was heated, the red wool coat would come in handy, inside, as well as out.

It was a fabulous and intriguing place, she decided as she crested the hill. All those flecks of mica in the stone, glinting like glass in the sunlight, made up for the boarded windows. The porches sagged, but the building itself rose up tall and proud against the bitter blue sky.

She liked the way the east wing jutted off at a stern angle. The way the trio of chimneys speared from the roof as if waiting to belch smoke. She even liked the way the broken shutters hung drunkenly.

It needed tending, she thought, with an affection that surprised her. Someone to love it, and accept its character for what it was. Someone who would appreciate its strengths and understand its weaknesses.

She shook her head and laughed at herself. It sounded as though she were thinking of a man—one, perhaps, like Rafe MacKade—rather than a house.

She walked closer, through the deep, powdery drifts. Rocks and overgrown brush made uneven lumps in the snow, like children under blankets waiting to do mischief. Brambles were sneaky enough to grab at her trousers with sharp, wiry fingers. But once the lawn had been lush and green and vivid with flowers.

If Rafe had any vision, it would be again.

Reminding herself that the landscaping was his problem, she puffed her way to the broken front porch.

He was, she thought with a scowl, late.

Regan looked around, stomped her feet for warmth and glanced at her watch. The man could hardly expect her to stand out in the cold and the wind and wait. Ten minutes, tops, she told herself. Then she would leave him a note, a very firm note on the value of keeping appointments, and leave.

But it wouldn't hurt to take a peek in the window.

Maneuvering carefully, she inched her way up the steps, avoided broken planks. There should be wisteria or morning glories climbing up the side arbor, she mused, and for a moment she almost believed she could catch the faint, sweet scent of spring.

She caught herself moving to the door, closing her hand over the knob before she realized that had been her intention all along. Surely it was locked, she thought. Even small towns weren't immune to vandals. But even as she thought it, the knob turned freely in her hand.

It was only sensible to go in, out of the wind, begin to site the job. Yet she pulled her hand back with a jerk. Her breath was coming in gasps, shockingly loud on the silent air. Inside her neat leather gloves, her hands were icy and trembling.

Out of breath from the climb, she told herself. Shivering from the wind. That was all. But the fear was on her like a cat, hissing through her blood.

Embarrassed, she looked uneasily around. There was no one to see her ridiculous reaction. Only snow and trees.

She took a deep breath, laughed at herself, and opened the door.

It creaked, of course. That was to be expected. The wide main hall gave her such a rush of pleasure, she forgot everything else. Closing the door, she leaned back against it and sighed.

There was dust and mold, damp patches on the walls, baseboards ruined by gnawing mice, spiderwebs draped like filthy gauze. She saw rich, deep green paint, creamy ivory trim, the buff and shine of waxed pine floors under her feet, a runner blooming with cabbage roses.

And there, she thought a hunt table, with a Dresden bowl spilling more roses, flanked by silver candlesticks. A little walnut hall chair with a pierced back, a hammered brass umbrella stand, a gilded mirror.

How it had been, and could be, spun through her mind, and she didn't feel the cold that sent her breath ahead of her in clouds as she wandered.

In the parlor, she marveled over the Adam fireplace. The marble was filthy, but undamaged. She had twin vases in the shop that would be perfect for the mantel. And a needlepoint footstool that was meant for weary feet in front of this very hearth.

Delighted, she pulled out her notebook and got to work.

Cobwebs dragged through her hair, dirt smudged her cheek, dust covered her boots, as she measured and plotted. She was in heaven. Her mood was so high that when she heard the footsteps, she turned with a smile instead of a complaint.

"It's wonderful. I can hardly—" She was talking to thin air.

Frowning, she walked out of the parlor and into the hall. She started to call out, then noted that there were no footprints in the dust but her own.

Imagining things, she told herself, and shuddered. Big, empty houses made all sorts of noises. Settling wood, wind against the windows...rodents, she thought with a grimace. She wasn't afraid of mice or spiders or creaking boards.

But when the floor groaned over her head, she couldn't muffle the shriek. Her heart flew straight to her throat and beat like a bird's. Before she'd managed to compose herself again, she heard the unmistakable sound of a door closing.

She was across the hall in a dash, fumbling for the knob when it hit her.

Rafe MacKade.

Oh, he thought he was clever, she thought furiously. Sneaking into the house ahead of her, creeping through the back, she imagined. He was up there right now, doubled over at the idea of her bolting from the house like some idiotic Gothic heroine with a heaving bosom.

Not on your life, she thought determinedly, and straightened her shoulders. She thrust her chin up and marched to the curving stairs.

"You're not funny, MacKade," she called out. "Now, if you've finished your pathetic little joke, I'd like to get some work done."

When the cold spot hit her, she was too shocked to move. The hand she'd gripped on the rail went numb with it, her face froze with it. There, halfway up the graceful sweep of stairs, she swayed. It was her own whimper that broke her free. She was up to the first landing in four effortless strides.

A draft, she told herself, cursing her own sobbing breaths. Just a nasty draft.

"Rafe." Her voice broke, infuriating her. Biting her lip, she stared down the long hallway, at the closed and secretive doors that lined it. "Rafe," she said again, and struggled to put irritation in her voice, rather than nerves. "I have a schedule to keep, even if you don't, so can we get on with this?"

The sound of wood scraping wood, the violent slam of a door, and a woman's heartbroken weeping. Pride forgotten, Regan flew down the stairs. She'd nearly reached the bottom when she heard the shot.

Then the door she'd rushed to meet groaned slowly open.

The room whirled once, twice, then vanished.

"Come on, darling, snap out of it."

Regan turned her head, moaned, shivered.

"All the way out, pal. Open those big blue eyes for me."

The voice was so coaxing, she did. And found herself looking into Rafe's.

"It wasn't funny."

A bit dizzy with relief, he smiled and stroked her cheek. "What wasn't?"

"Hiding upstairs to scare me." She blinked to bring the world back into sharp focus and discovered she was cradled on his lap on the window seat in the parlor. "Let me up."

"I don't think so. You're still a little shaky on your pins. Just relax a minute." He shifted her expertly so that her head rested in the crook of his arm.

"I'm fine."

"You're white as a sheet. If I had a flask, I'd pour some brandy into you. Never saw a woman faint as gracefully, though. You sort of drifted down, gave me a chance to catch you before your head knocked against the floor."

"If you expect me to thank you, forget it." She shoved, found him unmovable. "It's your fault."

"Thanks. It's flattering to think the sight of me has a woman dropping at my feet. There." He traced a finger down her cheek again. "That brought some color back."

"If this is the way you do business, you can take your job and—" She ground her teeth. "Let me up."

"Let's try this." Lifting her, he plopped her down

on the seat beside him. "Hands off," he added, lifting his. "Now why don't you tell me why you're ticked off at me?"

Pouting, she brushed at her smudged trousers. "You know very well."

"All I know is, I walked in the door and saw you doing a swan dive."

"I've never fainted in my life." And she was thoroughly mortified that she had done so now—in front of him. "If you want me to work on this house, scaring me into unconsciousness isn't the way to do it."

He studied her, reached into his pocket for the cigarettes he'd given up exactly eight days before. "How did I scare you?"

"By walking around upstairs, opening and closing doors, making those ridiculous noises."

"Maybe I should start off by telling you I got held up at the farm. I didn't leave until fifteen minutes ago."

"I don't believe you."

"I don't blame you." If he wasn't going to smoke, he had to move. Rising, he strolled over to the hearth. He thought he caught a whiff of smoke, as from a fire that had recently died. "Shane was there—and so was Cy Martin. He's mayor now."

"I know who Cy Martin is," she said testily.

"You should have known him in high school," Rafe mused. "He was a complete ass. Anyway, Cy dropped by to see if Shane could plow his lane. He was still there when I left. Fifteen minutes ago. I borrowed Shane's four-wheel to make the hill. Parked it and came to the door in time to see your eyes roll back in your head."

He walked back to her, stripped off his coat and tucked it over her legs. "By the way, how'd you get in?"

"I—" She stared at him, swallowed. "I opened the door."

"It was locked."

"No, it wasn't."

Lifting a brow, he jingled the keys in his pocket. "That's interesting."

"You're not lying," she said after a moment.

"Not this time. Why don't you tell me what you heard?"

"Footsteps. But there was no one there." To warm them, she tucked her hands under his coat. "Boards creaking upstairs. I started up. It was cold, bitterly cold, and it frightened me, so I went to the landing."

"You were scared, so you went up instead of out?"

"I thought you were up there. I was going to yell at you." Her smile was weak, but it was there. "I was furious that you'd managed to make me jump. Then I looked down the hallway. I guess I knew you weren't there. I heard wood scrape, and a door slam hard and someone crying. Then I bolted."

He sat beside her again, put his arm around her shoulders in a friendly squeeze. "Who wouldn't?"

"A shot," she remembered. "I was almost down the stairs when I heard a gunshot. It made my ears ring. Then the door opened, and lights-out."

"I shouldn't have been late." Unexpectedly, he leaned over and gave her a quick, casual kiss. "Sorry."

"That's hardly the point."

"The thing is, some people feel things in this place, some don't. You struck me as the cool, practical type."

She folded her arms over her chest. "Oh, really?"

"Single-minded," he added with a grin. "It seems you have more imagination than I expected. Feeling better now?"

"I'm fine."

"Sure you don't want to sit on my lap again?"

"Quite sure, thank you."

With his eyes on hers, he brushed a cobweb from her hair. "Want to get out of here?"

"Absolutely."

He picked up his coat. "I'd like to take you somewhere."

"That isn't necessary. I said I was…" She stood and, as he held his ground, bumped into his chest. "Fine," she managed.

"Business, darling." He tucked her hair behind her ear, flicked a finger over the square-cut aquamarine at the lobe. "For the moment. I think we can find someplace a little warmer and more hospitable to hash out the details."

That was reasonable, she decided. Perfectly sensible. "All right."

She picked up her briefcase and walked ahead of him to the door.

"Regan?"

"Yes?"

"Your face is dirty." He laughed at the smoldering look she shot at him, then scooped her up in his arms. Even as she stuttered a protest, he carried her over the broken porch. "Got to watch your step," he told her, setting her on her feet next to a Jeep.

"I make a habit of it."

"I bet you do," he murmured as he rounded the hood.

He maneuvered his way down the lane, circled around her car and kept going.

"I thought I'd follow you," she began.

"Since I don't think you mean to the ends of the earth, let's just take one car. I'll bring you back."

"From?"

"Home, sweet home, darling."

In the snow, with the sun glazing the white fields, the MacKade farm was Currier and Ives pretty. A stone house with covered porch, an arched roof on the red barn, weathered outbuildings and a pair of golden dogs, barking and yipping and kicking up snow completed the scene—one that appealed to Regan.

She'd driven past the MacKade place countless times—when the fields were brown and furrowed from the plow, when they were high with hay and corn. She'd even stopped once or twice when Shane was riding his tractor, and thought how completely suited he seemed to be to the land.

She couldn't picture Rafe MacKade in the same scene.

"You didn't come back to farm, I imagine."

"Hell, no. Shane loves it, Devin tolerates it. Jared looks on it as an ongoing enterprise."

She tilted her head as he parked the Jeep beside his car. "And you?"

"Hate it."

"No ties to the land?"

"I didn't say that. I said I hated farming." Rafe hopped out of the Jeep, clucking at the leaping golden retrievers. Before Regan could step down into the foot-deep snow, he'd plucked her up.

"I wish you'd stop that. I'm perfectly capable of walking through a little snow."

"City boots. Pretty enough, though," he commented as he carried her onto the porch. "You've got little feet. Stay out," he ordered the dogs. Smoothly he opened the door, elbowed it aside and carried her in.

"Hey, Rafe, what you got there?"

Grinning, Rafe shifted Regan in his arms and winked at Shane. "Got me a female."

"Good-looking one, too." Shane tossed the log he held onto the fire, straightened. His eyes, the color of fog over seawater, warmed in appreciation. "Hi there, Regan."

"Shane."

"Any coffee hot?" Rafe asked.

"Sure." Shane kicked the log into place with his boot. "Kitchen's never closed."

"Fine. Now get lost."

"Well, that was certainly rude." Regan blew her hair out of her eyes as Rafe carted her down the hall and into the kitchen.

"You're an only child, right?"

"Yes, but—"

"Figured." He dropped her into one of the cane chairs at the kitchen table. "What do you take in your coffee?"

"Nothing—black."

"What a woman." He stripped off his coat, tossed it over a peg by the back door, where his brother's heavy work jacket already hung. From a glass-fronted cupboard, he chose two glossy white mugs. "Want anything to go with it? Some hopeful woman's always baking Shane cookies. It's that pretty, innocent face of his."

"Pretty, maybe. You're all pretty." She shrugged out of her coat with a murmur of appreciation for the warmth of the room. "And I'll pass on the cookies."

He set a steaming mug in front of her. Out of habit, he turned a chair around and straddled it. "So, are you going to pass on the house, too?"

Biding her time, she studied her coffee, sampled it, and found it superb. "I have a number of pieces in stock that I think you'll find more than suitable when you're ready to furnish. I also did some research on the traditional color schemes and fabrics from that era."

"Is that a yes or a no, Regan?"

"No, I'm not going to pass." She lifted her gaze to his. "And it's going to cost you."

"You're not worried?"

"I didn't say that, exactly. But now I know what to expect. I can guarantee I won't be fainting at your feet a second time."

"I'd just as soon you didn't. You scared the life out of me." He reached over to play with the fingers of the hand she'd laid on the table. He liked the delicacy of them, and the glint of stones and gold. "In your research, did you dig up anything on the two corporals?"

"The two corporals?"

"You should have asked old lady Metz. She loves telling the story. What kind of watch is this?" Curious, Rafe flicked a finger under the twin black elastic bands.

"Circa 1920. Elastic and marcasite. What about the corporals?"

"It seems these two soldiers got separated from their regiments during the battle. The cornfield east of here was thick with smoke, black powder exploding. Some of the troops were engaged in the trees, others just lost or dying there."

"Some of the battle took place here, on your fields?" she asked.

"Some of it. The park service has markers up. Anyway, these two, one Union, one Confederate, got separated. They were just boys, probably terrified. Bad luck brought them together in the woods that form the boundary between MacKade land and Barlow."

"Oh." Thoughtful, she dragged her hair back. "I'd forgotten the properties border each other."

"It's less than a half mile from this house to the

Barlow place through the trees. Anyway, they came face-to-face. If either of them had had any sense, they'd have run for cover and counted their blessings. But they didn't." He lifted his mug again. "They managed to put holes in each other. Nobody can say who crawled off first. The Reb made it as far as the Barlow house. Odds are he was half-dead already, but he managed to crawl onto the porch. One of the servants saw him and, being a Southern sympathizer, pulled him inside. Or maybe she just saw a kid bleeding to death and did what she thought was right."

"And he died in the house," Regan murmured, wishing she couldn't see it so clearly.

"Yeah. The servant ran off to get her mistress. That was Abigail O'Brian Barlow, of the Carolina O'Brians. Abigail had just given orders for the boy to be taken upstairs, where she could treat his wounds. Her husband came out. He shot the kid, right there on the stairway."

Sadness jolted straight into horror. "Oh, my God! Why?"

"No wife of his was going to lay her hands on a Reb. She herself died two years later, in her room. Story is that she never spoke a word to her husband again—

not that they had much to say to each other before. It was supposed to be one of those arranged marriages. Rumor was he liked to knock her around."

"In other words," Regan said tightly, "he was a prince among men."

"That's the story. She was delicate, and she was miserable."

"And trapped," Regan murmured, thinking of Cassie.

"I don't suppose people talked much about abuse back then. Divorce…" He shrugged. "Probably not an option in her circumstances. Anyway, shooting that boy right in front of her must have been the straw, you know. The last cruelty she could take. But that's only half of it. The half the town knows."

"There's more." She let out a sigh and rose. "I think I need more coffee."

"The Yank stumbled off in the opposite direction," Rafe continued, murmuring a thank you when she poured him a second cup. "My great-grandfather found him passed out by the smokehouse. My great-grandfather lost his oldest son at Bull Run—he'd died wearing Confederate gray."

Regan shut her eyes. "He killed the boy."

"No. Maybe he thought about it, maybe he thought

about just leaving him there to bleed to death. But he picked him up and brought him into the kitchen. He and his wife, their daughters, doctored him on the table. Not this one," Rafe added with a small smile.

"That's reassuring."

"He came around a few times, tried to tell them something. But he was too weak. He lasted the rest of that day and most of the night, but he was dead by morning."

"They'd done everything they could."

"Yeah, but now they had a dead Union soldier in their kitchen, his blood on their floor. Everyone who knew them knew that they were staunch Southern sympathizers who'd already lost one son to the cause and had two more still fighting for it. They were afraid, so they hid the body. When it was dark, they buried him, with his uniform, his weapon, and a letter from his mother in his pocket."

He looked at her then, his eyes cool and steady. "That's why this house is haunted, too. I thought you'd be interested."

She didn't speak for a moment, set her coffee aside. "Your house is haunted?"

"The house, the woods, the fields. You get used to

it, the little noises, the little feelings. We never talked about it much; it was just there. Maybe you'd get a sense of something in the woods at night, or in the fields, when the morning was misty and too quiet." He smiled a little at the curiosity in her eyes. "Even cynics feel something when they're standing on a battlefield. After my mother died, even the house seemed... restless. Or maybe it was just me."

"Is that why you left?"

"I had lots of reasons for leaving."

"And for coming back?"

"One or two. I told you the first part of the story because I figured you should understand the Barlow place, since you're going to be involved with it. And I told you the rest..." He reached over and loosened the duo of black buttons on her blazer. "Because I'm going to be staying at the farm for a while. Now you can decide if you want me to bring you here, or if you'd rather I come to your place."

"My inventory's at the shop, so—"

"I'm not talking about your inventory." He cupped her chin in his hand, kept his eyes open and on hers when he kissed her.

Softly at first, testing. Then with a murmur of satisfaction, deeper, so that her lips parted and warmed. He watched her lashes flutter, felt her breath sigh out and into his mouth, felt the pulse just under her jaw, just under his fingers, throb. The smoky scent of her skin was a seductive contrast to her cool-water taste.

Regan kept her hands gripped tight in her lap. It was shocking how much she wanted to use them on him. To drag them through his hair, to test the muscles under that faded flannel shirt. But she didn't. Her mind might have blurred for just an instant with astonished pleasure, even more astonishing greed, but she managed to hold on to her focus.

When he leaned back, she kept her hands where they were and gave herself time to level her voice. "We're business associates, not playmates."

"We have business," he agreed.

"Would you have pulled that maneuver if I'd been a man?"

He stared at her. The chuckle started low, bloomed into a full laugh while she squirmed at the ridiculous way she'd phrased the question.

"I can give you a definite no on that one. I figure in that case you probably wouldn't have kissed me back, either."

"Look, let's clear this up. I've heard all about the MacKade brothers and how they're irresistible to women."

"It's been a curse all our lives."

She would not smile—even if she had to clamp her teeth together. "The point is, I'm not interested in a quick roll, an affair, or a relationship—which should cover any and all possibilities."

Damned if she wasn't even more alluring when she went prim. "I'm going to enjoy changing your mind. Why don't we start with the quick roll and work our way up from there?"

She rose sharply and pulled her coat on. "In your dreams."

"You're right about that. Why don't I take you out to dinner?"

"Why don't you take me back to my car?"

"All right." Unoffended, he got up to pluck his coat from the peg. After he'd shrugged it on, he reached out and flipped her hair out from the collar of hers. "Nights are long and cold this time of year."

"Get a book," she suggested on her way down the hall. "Sit by the fire."

"Is that what you do?" He shook his head. "I'm going to have to add a little excitement to your life."

"I like my life just fine, thanks. Don't pick me—" The order ended with an oath as he scooped her up. "MacKade," she said with a sigh as he carried her to the Jeep, "I'm beginning to think you're as bad as everyone says."

"Count on it."

Chapter 3

It was a good sound. The thud of hammers, the buzz of saws, the whir of drills. Through it came the jingle of a radio set to country music, so that Wynonna wailed over the clomp of boots and male voices.

It was a noise, the music of labor, that Rafe had known all of his life. This was different from the clatter of the milking barn, the hum of a tractor in the field. He preferred it. He'd chosen it the day he left Antietam.

Construction work had probably saved him. He had no problem admitting he'd been looking to rumble when he roared out of Washington County a decade before on his secondhand Harley. But he'd needed to eat, so he'd needed to work.

He'd strapped on a tool belt and sweated out the worst of the frustration.

He still remembered when he'd stepped back and looked at the first house he'd had a part in building. It had come to him in a flash that he could make something that mattered. And that he could make something of himself.

So he'd saved, and he'd sweated, and he'd learned.

The first place he'd bought, in central Florida, was little more than a shack. He'd choked on drywall dust, hammered until his muscles wept with the strain. But he'd made a profit, and used that to buy again. To sell again.

In four years, the tiny shoestring company called MacKade had earned a reputation for reliable, quality work.

Still, he'd never stopped looking back. Now, standing in the parlor of the Barlow place, he understood he'd come full circle.

He was going to make something in the town he'd been so hell-bent to escape from. Whether he stayed or not after he was done was undecided. But he would, at least, have left his mark.

Hunkered down in front of the fireplace, Rafe studied the stone hearth. He'd already gone to work on the chimney, and was covered with soot and grime. She'd draw, he thought with satisfaction. The first thing he was going to do, when the new lining was installed to bring it up to code, was build a fire. He wanted to watch the flames and warm his hands on them.

He wanted just the right andirons, the right screen. He could depend on Regan for that.

With a little smile, he picked up his trowel to mix a bucket of mortar. He had a feeling Regan could be depended on for most anything.

With care, precision and enjoyment, he began to repoint the stone.

"I figured the boss would be sitting at a desk, running figures."

Rafe glanced back and lifted a brow. Jared stood in the center of the room, his gleaming black shoes resting on a spattered drop cloth. For some reason, his black Wayfarer shades didn't look out of place with his gray pin-striped three-piece suit.

"That stuff's for lawyers and bookkeepers."

Jared took off the sunglasses and tucked them into the pocket of his suit jacket. "And think what the world would be without them."

"Simpler." Rafe stuck his trowel in the mortar and gave his brother a once-over. "On your way to a funeral?"

"I had business in town, thought I'd drop by and see how things are going." He glanced around the room, then back toward the hall when something crashed, someone cursed. "So, how's it going?"

"Steady." Rafe sighed when Jared took out a slim cigar. "Blow some of that over here, will you? I quit ten really long days ago."

"Reforming yourself?" Obligingly, Jared walked over, crouched. He smoked lazily as he and Rafe frowned meaningfully at the stone. "Not too shabby."

Rafe knocked a fist against the rose-grained marble. "An Adam, pal."

Jared grunted, clamped the cigar between his teeth. "Need a hand around here?"

Blandly Rafe looked down. "You're wearing your lawyer shoes."

"I meant over the weekend."

"I can always use another back." Pleased with the offer, Rafe picked up the trowel again. "How's yours?"

"As good as yours."

"Still working out?" He gave Jared's biceps a testing punch. "I still say gyms are for sissies."

Jared blew out a stream of smoke. "Want to go a round, bro?"

"Sure, when you're not dressed so pretty." To torture himself, Rafe sucked in secondhand smoke. "I appreciate you handling the settlement on this place for me."

"You haven't got my bill, yet." Grinning, Jared straightened. "I thought you were crazy when you called and told me to go after it. Then I did a walk-through." He turned, still grinning. "And I knew you were crazy. You practically stole the place, but I figure it's got to cost you two times the purchase price to make it livable."

"Three times," Rafe said mildly, "to make it the way I want it."

"How do you want it?"

"The way it was." Rafe scraped the edge of his trowel over stone, leveling his mortar.

"That's always a tough one," Jared murmured. "You

don't seem to be having a problem with labor. I wondered if you would, considering the place's rep."

"Money talks. Lost a plumber's assistant this morning, though." Wicked amusement sparkled in his eyes. "They were checking pipes in one of the second-floor johns. This guy claims someone clamped a hand on his shoulder. He was still running when he made it to the road. Don't guess he'll be back."

"Any other problems?"

"Nothing I need a lawyer for. Did you hear the one about the lawyer and the rattlesnake?"

"I've heard them all," Jared said dryly. "I keep a file."

With a chuckle, Rafe wiped his hands on his jeans. "You did good, Jare. Mom would've liked seeing you duded up like that." For a moment, he said nothing. There was only the scrape of trowel on stone. "It's weird, staying at the farm. Mostly just me and Shane. Devin spends half his nights on a cot in the sheriff's office. You're in that fancy little town house in the city. When I hear Shane get up in the morning, it's still dark. The idiot's whistling, like going out to milk in January's just a boatload of laughs."

"He's always loved it. He's kept that place alive."

"I know."

He recognized the tone, shook his head at it. "You did your part, Rafe. The money you sent back made a difference." Eyes shadowed, Jared stared out the grimy window. "I'm thinking of selling the place in Hagerstown." When Rafe said nothing, Jared moved his shoulders. "It seemed practical to keep it after the divorce. The market was soft, and we'd only built up a couple years' equity. Barbara didn't want it."

"Still sore?"

"No. The divorce is three years past, and God knows it was civilized. We just didn't like each other anymore."

"I never liked her."

Jared's lips quirked. "I know. Anyway, I'm thinking of selling, hanging out at the farm for a while, until I find the right place."

"Shane would like that. So would I. I missed you." Rafe swiped a grimy hand over his grimy chin. "I didn't realize how much until I got back." Satisfied with the repointing, he scraped his trowel on the edge of the bucket. "So, you want to put in some honest labor on Saturday?"

"You buy the beer."

Rafe nodded, rose. "Let's see your hands, city boy."

Jared's response was crude, simple, and uttered just as Regan stepped into the room.

"Nice mouth, Counselor," Rafe said with an easy smile. "Hello, darling."

"I'm interrupting."

"No. The guy from the gutter here's my brother Jared."

"I know. He's my lawyer. Hello, Jared."

"Regan." Jared found an empty can of soda and doused the stub of his cigar. "How's business?"

"Picking up, thanks to your little brother. I have some estimates, figures, suggestions, paint and fabric samples," she said to Rafe. "I thought you'd like to look them over."

"You've been busy." He crouched again, flipped over the top of a small cooler. "Want a drink?"

"No, thanks."

"Jare?"

"One for the road. I've got another appointment." Jared caught the canned soft drink on the fly, then took his sunglasses out of his pocket. "I'll let you two get down to business. Nice to see you again, Regan."

"Saturday," Rafe called out as Jared left the room. "Seven-thirty. That's a.m., pal. And lose the suit."

"I didn't mean to chase him off," Regan began.

"You didn't. Want to sit down?"

"Where?"

He patted an overturned bucket.

"That's very gracious of you, but I can't stay. I'm on my lunch hour."

"The boss isn't going to dock you."

"She certainly will." Opening her briefcase, Regan took out two thick folders. "Everything's in here. Once you have a chance to look through it, let me know." For lack of anywhere better, she set the files across two sawhorses. She looked back over her shoulder, toward the hall. "You've certainly jumped right in."

"When you know what you want, there's no point in wasting time. So how about dinner?"

She looked back, narrowed her eyes. "Dinner?"

"Tonight. We can go over your files." He tapped a finger against them, left a smudge of soot. "Save time."

"Oh." Still frowning, she combed her fingers through her hair. "I suppose."

"How's seven? We'll go to the Lamplighter."

"The where?"

"The Lamplighter. The little place off of Main, at Church Street."

She tilted her head as she visualized the town. "There's a video store at Main and Church."

He jammed his hands in his pockets with an oath. "Used to be a restaurant. Your place used to be a hardware store."

"I guess even small towns have their changes."

"Yeah." He couldn't have said why it annoyed him. "Like Italian?"

"Yes. But the closest Italian place is across the river, into West Virginia. We can just meet at Ed's."

"No. Italian. I'll come by about six-thirty." Needing to gauge his time, he pulled a watch from his pocket. "Yeah, I can do six-thirty."

"That's a nice one." Without thinking, she crossed over, took his wrist gingerly in two fingers to get a better look at the pocket watch. "Hmm...American Watch Company, mid-1800s." Already appraising, she turned the watch over to study the case. "Sterling, good condition. I'll give you seventy-five for it."

"I paid ninety."

She laughed and shook back her hair. "Then you got a hell of a bargain. It's worth a hundred and fifty."

Her gaze danced up to his. "You don't look like the pocket-watch type."

"Wear one on your wrist on the job, they end up smashed." He wanted to touch her. She looked so neat and tidy that the idea of mussing her up was enormously appealing. "Damn shame my hands are filthy."

Alerted, she released his wrist, brushed one hand against the other. "So's your face. But you're still pretty." After shifting her briefcase strap more comfortably on her shoulder, she stepped back. "Six-thirty, then. Don't forget the files."

She'd changed three times before she caught herself. A business dinner, Regan thought as she dropped down on the padded stool of her vanity, was a business dinner. Her appearance was certainly important, but it was secondary.

She bit her lip and wondered if she should have gone with the little black dress, after all.

No, no, no. Annoyed with herself, she snatched up her brush. Simplicity was best. The restaurant in West Virginia was casual, family-style. The purpose was professional. The blazer, slacks and silk blouse in forest green were right. There was no harm in jazzing it up with the moonstone lapel pin. But maybe the earrings were wrong. She could go with plain gold hoops instead of the more dramatic dangles.

The hell with it. She dropped her brush, then tugged on her suede ankle boots. She would not fall into the trap of thinking of this as a date. She didn't want to date Rafe MacKade. Just now, with her business showing real promise, she didn't want to date anyone.

A relationship, if indeed she decided to cultivate one, was three years down the road. Minimum. She would never make the mistake her mother had and depend on someone else for emotional and financial support. First, she would make certain she was solvent, solid and secure. And then, if and when she chose, she would think about sharing her life.

No one was going to tell her if she could work or not. She would never have to cajole an extra few dollars out of a man to buy a new dress. Maybe it suited her parents to live that way—and they'd certainly always seemed happy enough. But that wasn't the life Regan Bishop wanted.

It was just too damned bad that Rafe was so dangerously attractive. And, she noted when she heard the knock on the door, prompt.

Confident again after the quick pep talk, she walked out of the bedroom, through the small, cozily furnished living room, and opened the door.

And, oh, she thought one last time, it was really too bad.

He flashed that grin at her, and those wonderful green eyes swept down, then up. "Looking good." Before she could think to avoid it, his mouth brushed hers.

"I'll get my coat," she began, then stopped, the door still open to the wind. "What are those?"

"These?" He jostled the bags he carried. "These are dinner. Where's your kitchen?"

"I—" He was already in, kicking the door behind him. "I thought we were going out."

"No, I said we were having Italian." He took quick stock of the room. Lady chairs, gleaming tables, pretty little knickknacks and fresh flowers. All female, he mused. And the portrait of a gloomy-faced cow above the sofa added wit. "Nice place."

"Are you telling me you're cooking me dinner?"

"It's the quickest way, without physical contact, to get a woman into bed. The kitchen through there?"

When she'd managed to close her mouth, she followed him into the galley-style kitchen off the dining el. "Doesn't that depend on how well you cook?"

Appreciating her response, he smiled as he began pulling ingredients out of the bags. "You'll have to tell me. Got a skillet?"

"Yes, I have a skillet." She took a large cast-iron pan from its cupboard, then lips pursed, tapped it against her palm.

"You conk me with it, you'll miss out on my ziti with tomato and basil."

"Ziti?" After running her tongue around her teeth, she set the skillet on a burner. "I'll wait until after I eat." She got out a second pot for the pasta and handed it to him.

Once he'd added water and set it to boil, she watched him wash greens for a salad.

"Where'd you learn to cook?"

"We all cook. Chef's knife? My mother didn't believe there was women's work and men's work. Thanks," he added and began chopping with a quick, negligent flair that had Regan lifting her brows. "There was just work," he continued.

"Ziti doesn't sound like farm food."

"She had an Italian grandmother. Can you stand a little closer?"

"Hmm?"

"You smell good. I like to smell you."

Ignoring that, and the little twist in her stomach, she picked up the wine he'd brought along. "Why don't I open this?"

"Why don't you?"

After she'd set it on the counter to breathe, she scooted behind him to reach the cupboard to get a salad bowl. When he asked for music, she slipped back into the living room and put Count Basie on low. Why, she wondered, did a man look so sexy with his sleeves rolled up, grating carrots into a salad?

"Don't open that olive oil," she told him. "I have some."

"Extra virgin?"

"Of course." She tapped a long-spouted copper pitcher on the counter.

"Count Basie, your own olive oil." His eyes met hers, laughed. "Want to get married?"

"Sure. I've got time on Saturday." Amused that he didn't have such a quick comeback for that, she reached overhead for wineglasses.

"I was planning on working Saturday." Watching her, he set the salad aside.

"That's what they all say."

Lord, she was one terrific piece of work. He moved closer as she poured the wine. "Tell me you like watching baseball on TV on hot summer nights, and we've got a deal."

"Sorry. I hate sports."

He moved closer still, and with a wineglass in either hand, she moved back. "It's a good thing I found this flaw now, before we had five or six kids and a dog."

"You're a lucky guy." Heart jittering, she backed up again.

"I like this," he murmured, and traced a finger over the little mole beside her mouth. Inching closer, he ran his finger down to flip open the buttons of her blazer.

"Why are you always doing that?"

"Doing what?"

"Fooling with my buttons."

"Just practicing." The grin was quick as lightning, and just as bold. "Besides, you always look so tidy, I can't resist loosening you up."

Her retreat ended with her back between the side of the refrigerator and the wall.

"Looks like you've backed yourself into a corner, darling."

He moved in slowly, slipping his hands around her waist, fitting his mouth to hers. He took his time sampling, his fingers spread over her rib cage, stopping just short of the curve of her breasts.

She couldn't stop her breath from quickening or her lips from responding. His tongue flicked over them, between them, met hers. His taste was dark, and rabidly male, and streaked straight to her center like an arrow on target.

The small part of her mind that could still function warned her that he knew exactly how he affected women. All women. Any woman. But her body didn't seem to give a damn.

Her blood began to pound, her skin to vibrate, from the shock of dozens of tiny explosions. She was certain she could feel her own bones melt.

She was exciting to watch. His eyes were open as he changed the angle of the kiss, deepened it, degree by painfully slow degree. He found the flutter of her lashes arousing, the faint flush desire brought to her cheeks seductive. And that helpless hitch of breath, that quick shiver when his fingers skimmed lightly over the tips of her breasts, utterly thrilling.

With an effort, he stopped himself from taking more. "God. It gets better every time." Gently he nuzzled his way to her ear. "Let's try it again."

"No." It surprised her that what she said and what she wanted were entirely different. In defense, she pressed a wineglass against his chest.

He glanced down at the glass, then back at her face. His eyes weren't smiling now, weren't gently amused. There was an edge in them now, dark and potentially deadly. Despite all common sense, she found herself drawn to this man who would take, and damn all consequences.

"Your hand's shaking, Regan."

"I'm aware of that."

She spoke carefully, knowing that the wrong word, the wrong move, and what was in his eyes would leap out and devour her. And she would let it. She would love it.

That was something she definitely had to think over.

"Take the wine, Rafe. It's red. It'll leave a nasty stain on that shirt."

For one humming moment, he said nothing. A need he hadn't understood or counted on had him by the throat with rusty little claws. She was afraid of him, he noted, deciding she was smart to be afraid. A woman like her didn't have a clue what a man like him was really capable of.

Taking the glass, he tapped it against hers, making the crystal ring, then turned back to the stove.

She felt as though she'd barely avoided a tumble from a cliff. And realized she already regretted not taking the plunge. "I think I should say something. I, um…" She took a deep breath, then an even deeper gulp of wine. "I'm not going to pretend I'm not attracted to you, or that I didn't enjoy that, when obviously I am, and I did."

Trying to relax, he leaned back against the counter, studied her over the rim of his glass. "And?"

"And." She scooped back her hair. "And I think complications are…complicated," she said lamely. "I don't want—that is, I don't think…" She shut her eyes and drank again. "I'm stuttering."

"I noticed. It's a nice boost to the ego."

"Your ego doesn't need any boosting." She blew out a breath, cleared her throat. "You're very potent. I have no doubt sex would be memorable— Don't smile at me that way."

"Sorry." But the smile didn't dim. "It must have been your choice of words. *Memorable*'s good. I like it. Why don't we save time here? I get your point. You want to mull the idea over, make the next move when you're ready."

She considered, then nodded slowly. "That's close enough."

"Okay. Now here's my point." He turned on the burner under the skillet and added oil. "I really want you, Regan. It hit me right off, when I walked into Ed's and you were sitting there with little Cassie, looking so pressed and polished."

She fought to ignore the flutters in her stomach. "Is that why you offered me the job on the Barlow place?"

"You're too smart to ask a question like that. This is sex. Sex is personal."

"All right." She nodded again. "All right."

He picked up a plump roma tomato, examined it. "The problem here, as I see it, is that I don't much care for mulling over things like this. No matter how you fancy it up, sex is still the animal. Smell, touch, taste."

His eyes were dark again, reckless. He picked up the

knife, tested its point. "Take," he added. "But that's just me, and there are two of us here. So you go on ahead with your mulling."

Baffled, she stared at him as he chose a clove of garlic. "I'm trying to decide if you expect me to thank you for that."

"Nope." Expertly he laid the flat of his knife over the garlic, gave one quick pound of his fist to crush it. "You're just supposed to understand it, like I'm understanding you."

"You're a real nineties man, MacKade."

"No, I'm not. And I'm going to make you stutter again. You can count on that."

Challenged, she picked up the wine, topped off their glasses. "Well, you count on this. If and when I decide to make my move, you'll do some stuttering of your own."

He scooped the minced garlic into the oil, where it sizzled. "I like your style, darling. I really like your style."

Chapter 4

Sunny skies and a southerly breeze brought in a welcome end-of-January thaw. Icicles dripped prettily from eaves and shone with rainbows. In front yards and fallow fields, snowmen began to lose weight. Regan spent a pleasant week earmarking stock for the Barlow place and hunting up additions to her supply at auction.

When business was slow, she revised and honed her room-by-room decorating scheme for what was going to be the MacKade Inn at Antietam.

Even now, as she described the attributes of a walnut credenza to a pair of very interested buyers, her mind was on the house. Though she hadn't realized it, yet, she was as haunted by it as Rafe had been.

The front bedroom, second floor, she mused, should have the four-poster with canopy, the rosebud wallpaper and the satinwood armoire. A romantic and traditional bridal suite, complete with little bowls of potpourri and vases of fresh flowers.

And what had been the gathering room, on the main level, had that wonderful southern exposure. Of course, Rafe had to pick the right windows, but it would be spectacular in sunny colors with a trio of ficus trees, hanging ferns in glazed pots, and pretty little conversation groups of boldly floral love seats and wingback chairs.

It was perfect for a conservatory, a place to gaze through the glass into the woods and gardens, with forced narcissi and hyacinths brightening midwinter gloom.

She couldn't wait to get her hands on the place, add those tiny, perfect details that would make it a home again.

An inn, she reminded herself. A business. Comfortable, charming, but temporary. And it wasn't hers.

With an effort, she shook her head clear and concentrated on the sale at hand.

"You can see the marquetry is high-quality," she continued, keeping her sales pitch moderate and pleasant. "The bowfront cupboards on the side are the original glass."

The woman fingered the discreet tag longingly, and Regan's sharp eye caught the hopeful glance she sent her less enthusiastic husband.

"It really is lovely. But it's just a little more than we had in mind."

"I understand. But in this condition—"

She broke off when the door opened, furious with herself for the quick leap, then the quick disappointment when it wasn't Rafe who came in. Before she could smile a welcome at Cassie, she saw the livid bruises on the side of her friend's face.

"If you'd excuse me for just a moment, I'll give you time to talk it over."

An antique bangle jingling on her wrist, sensible shoes clacking, she moved swiftly through the shop. Saying nothing, she took Cassie's arm and led her into the back room.

"Sit down. Come on." Gently, she eased Cassie into a chair at the tiny iron table. "How bad are you hurt?"

"It's nothing. I just—"

"Shut up." Grinding back the spurt of temper, Regan slammed a kettle on the hot plate. "I'm sorry. I'm going to make some tea." She needed a moment, she realized, before she could deal with this rationally. "While the water's boiling, I'll go finish up with my customers. You sit here and relax for a minute."

Shame swimming in her eyes, Cassie stared down at her hands. "Thanks."

Ten minutes later, after ruthlessly hacking the price of the credenza to move the customers along, Regan hurried back. She told herself she'd gotten the anger under control. She promised herself she would be supportive, sympathetic.

One look at Cassie, slumped in the chair while the kettle belched steam, had her exploding.

"Why in the hell do you let him do this to you? When are you going to get tired of being that sadistic bastard's punching bag? Does he have to put you in the hospital before you walk away?"

In utter defeat, Cassie folded her arms on the table, then dropped her head on them and wept.

Her own eyes stinging, Regan dropped to her knees beside the chair. In the tidy little office, with its ice-cream-parlor chairs and neat rolltop desk, she struggled to face the reality of battering.

"Cassie, I'm sorry. I'm so sorry, Cass. I shouldn't be yelling at you."

"I shouldn't have come here." Lifting her head, Cassie covered her face with her hand and fought to get her breath back. "I shouldn't have come. But I just needed somebody to talk to."

"Of course you should have come here. This is exactly where you should have come. Let me see," Regan murmured, easing Cassie's hand away. The bruises ran from temple to jaw, in ugly purple. One of Cassie's lovely smoke gray eyes was swollen nearly shut.

"Oh, Cassie, what happened? Can you tell me?"

"He…Joe…he hasn't been feeling well. This flu that's been going around." Cassie's voice hitched and jittered. "He missed a lot of work, being sick, and yesterday they laid him off."

Avoiding Regan's eyes, she fumbled in her bag for a tissue. "He was upset—he's worked there almost twelve years now, on and off. The bills. I just bought a new washing machine on credit, and Connor wanted these new tennis shoes. I knew they were too expensive, but—"

"Stop," Regan said quietly, and laid a hand over Cassie's. "Please stop blaming yourself. I can't bear it when you do."

"I know I'm making excuses." With a long, shuddering breath, Cassie shut her eyes. To Regan, at least, she could be honest. Because Regan, in the three years they had known each other, had always been there. "He hasn't had the flu. He's been drunk almost day and night for a week. They didn't lay him off, they fired him because he went to work drunk and mouthed off to his supervisor."

"And then he came home and took it out on you." Rising, Regan took the kettle off the hot plate and began to make the tea. "Where are the kids?"

"At my mother's. I went there last night, after. He hurt me pretty bad this time."

Unconsciously she touched her hand to her throat. Beneath the turtleneck there were more bruises, where Joe's hands had held and choked her until she accepted that he would kill her. Almost wished for it.

"I got the kids out, and I went to Mama, because I needed some place to stay."

"Okay, that's good." Ready to move step-by-step now, Regan brought two china cups to the table. "That's the best way to start."

"No." Very carefully, Cassie wrapped both hands around her cup. "She expects me to go back today. She won't let us stay another night."

"After you told her, after she saw you, what he'd done, she expects you to go back?"

"A woman belongs with her husband," Cassie said simply. "I married him for better or for worse."

Regan had never understood her own mother, the easy subservience, the catering. But, while it had infuriated her often, it had never appalled her like this.

"That's monstrous, Cassie."

"It's just Mama," Cassie murmured, wincing as the tea stung her puffy lip. "She believes a woman should make a marriage work. It's her duty to make it work."

"Do you believe that? That it's your responsibility to take this? Do you believe that means you are supposed to stay for better or worse, even if worse means being beaten whenever he has the whim?"

"I used to. I tried to. I took vows, Regan." She took a shuddering breath, because to her that had always been the bottom line. She had promised. "Maybe I was too young when I married Joe. Maybe I made a mistake, but I still took the vows. He didn't keep them. There were those other women, he didn't even care if I knew who they were. He was never faithful, never kind. But I took vows and I wanted to keep them."

She began to cry again, quietly now, because she had failed. "We've been married ten years. We have children together. I make so many mistakes—using my tip money to buy those shoes for Connor, and letting Emma play dress-up with my lipstick. And we couldn't afford that washing machine. I was never any good in bed, not like those other women he'd go to. I knew—"

She broke off when Regan only continued to watch her.

"Are you hearing yourself this time?" Regan said quietly. "Are you listening to yourself, Cassie?"

"I can't stay with him anymore." Her voice broke, shattering like thin, fragile glass. "He's hitting me in front of the kids. He used to wait until they were in bed, and that was bad. But now he hits me in front of them, and he says terrible things. Things they shouldn't hear. It's not right. It makes them part of it, and it's not right."

"No, Cass, it's not right. You need help now."

"I thought about it all night." She hesitated, then slowly eased down the neck of her sweater.

At the sight of the raw marks scoring that pale, innocent flesh, Regan's face went white and cold. "Oh, dear God—he tried to strangle you."

"I don't think he meant to at first. I was crying, and he wanted me to stop. But then he did." Cassie lowered her hand again. "I could see it in his eyes. It wasn't just the drinking, or the money, or the other women he seems to want. He hated me just for being there. He'll hurt me again if he gets the chance, and I have to think about the kids. I have to go to Devin and file charges."

"Thank God."

"I had to come here first, to get up my nerve." Knowing there was no more point in them, Cassie wiped at the tears. "It's hard, being it's Devin. I've known him all my life. It's not like it's a secret. He's been out to the house I don't know how many times when the neighbors called in. But it's hard." She sighed. "Being it's Devin."

"I'll go with you."

Cassie closed her eyes. That was why she had come

here, to have someone stand with her. No, she admitted, ashamed all over again. To have someone hold her up.

"No, I need to do it myself. I haven't thought about after," she said, and soothed her raw throat with a sip of tea. "I can't take the kids back to the house until I know what's going to happen."

"The shelter—"

Stubbornly, Cassie shook her head. "I know it's pride, Regan, but I can't go there. I can't take my kids there. Not yet, anyway."

"All right, then you'll stay here. Here," Regan repeated as Cassie protested. "I only have one extra bedroom, so you and the kids will have to rough it."

"We can't pile in on you that way."

"You were the first friend I made when I moved here. I want to help. So let me help."

"I could never ask you that, Regan. I've saved some tip and overtime money. Enough for a motel for a couple of days."

"You wouldn't want to hurt my feelings that way. You're going to stay at my place. For the kids," Regan murmured, knowing that nothing would tilt the scales as heavily.

"I'll go get them after I see Devin." She had no pride when it came to her children. "I'm awfully grateful, Regan."

"So am I. Now."

"What's this? Tea party during business hours?" Because his eyes were on Regan, Rafe had stepped into the office and tossed his coat over the back of a chair before he saw Cassie's face.

Regan was stunned to watch charm metamorphize into pure violence in a split second. The quick, potent grin sharpened into a snarl. His eyes fired. Her first startled thought, as that lean body tensed to spring, was *wolf*.

When his hand shot out, Cassie flinched, and Regan leapt to her feet. Before Regan could step between them with some wild idea of protecting Cassie, Rafe's fingers stroked, gentle as a kiss, over the battered face.

"Joe?"

"It—it was an accident," Cassie stammered.

His opinion of that was one vicious word. He swung around, blood in his eye. Cassie was on her feet and racing after him.

"No, Rafe, please don't do anything." Desperate, she

pulled at his arm, all but jumped on his back. "Please don't go after him."

He could have knocked her aside with a shrug. It was that knowledge that added bitter fuel to the fire. "You stay here. Stay with Regan."

"No, please." Cassie began to weep again, helplessly, as she pulled at him. "Please. Don't make me any more ashamed than I already am."

"The bastard's going to pay this time." He bit the words out, started to set her aside and looked down. The tears did what fists and threats could never have done. They stopped him cold. "Cassie." Undone, he wrapped his arms around her and cradled her against his chest. "Don't cry, baby. Come on now, it's going to be all right."

From the doorway of the office, Regan watched him. How could there be such tenderness, she wondered, side by side with such savagery? He was holding Cassie as though she were a child, his head close to hers as he murmured to her.

Regan's own throat burned, and her own cheeks were wet when he lifted his head and looked at her.

Yes, the violence was still there, alive and restless in his eyes. Vital and fierce enough to steal her breath from her throat and make her stomach muscles quiver. She swallowed hard before she spoke.

"Bring her back in here, Rafe. Please."

Every nerve inside him was tensed for battle. He craved the hunt, the fight, the blood. But the woman in his arms was trembling. And the one who watched him with shocked, frightened eyes was quietly pleading.

"Come on, baby." As if she were a fretful child, Rafe tucked Cassie under his arm. "Come on, let's go sit down."

"I'm sorry."

"Don't apologize to me." It took every ounce of control to lead her back into the office, to keep his voice easy on the words. "Don't apologize to anyone."

"She's going to Devin." Because her hands were shaking, Regan busied them with the tea and cups. "She's going to file charges. That's the right way to handle it."

"That's one way." He preferred his own, but he eased Cassie into a chair, brushed her hair way from her damp face. "Have you got a place to stay?"

Cassie nodded, took the tissues Regan handed her.

"We're going to stay with Regan for a little while. Just until..."

"The kids okay?"

She nodded again. "I'm going to get them as soon as I see Devin."

"You tell me what you need, and I'll go by the house and pick it up for you."

"I...I don't know. I didn't take anything."

"You tell me later. Why don't I walk you down to the sheriff's office?"

She shuddered out a breath, mopped her face. "No, I need to do it by myself. I should go now."

"Here." Regan pulled open a drawer in her desk. "Here's a key to the door upstairs. You and the kids settle in." She put the key in Cassie's hand, closed her fingers over it. "And lock it, Cassie."

"I will. I'll go now." It was the hardest thing she'd ever done, just standing, walking to the door. "I always thought it would get better," she said, almost to herself. "I always hoped it would." She left, with her head bowed and her shoulders hunched.

"Do you know where he is?" Rafe murmured.

"No, I don't."

"Well, I'll find him." As he reached for his coat,

Regan put her hand over his. His eyes lifted slowly to hers and burned. "Don't get in my way."

Instinct had her laying her other hand on his cheek, her mouth on his. The kiss was soft, soothing them both.

"What was that for?"

"A couple of things." She took a deep breath, then put both hands on his shoulders. "For wanting to kick the bastard's face in." She kissed him again. "For not doing it because Cassie asked you." And again. "And last, for showing her that most men, real men, are kind."

"Damn." Defeated, he laid his brow on hers. "That's a hell of a way to keep me from killing him."

"Part of me would like you to. I'm not proud of it." As the anger stirred again, she turned back to the hot plate. "Part of me would like to watch while you beat him senseless. Even worse, I'd like a shot at him myself."

Rafe stepped over, uncurled the hand she'd balled into a fist. Thoughtfully, he lifted it, pressed his lips to the palm. "Well, well... And I figured you for a cream puff."

"I said I'm not proud of it." But she smiled a little.

"It's not what she needs now. Violence is just what she needs to get away from. Even if it's justified."

"I've known her since she was a kid." Rafe glanced down at the tea Regan poured him, shook his head at it. It smelled like a meadow at springtime, and would undoubtedly taste the same.

"She was always little, pretty and shy. All this sweetness." At Regan's curious look, he shook his head again. "No. I never made any moves in that direction. Sweet's never been my type."

"Thanks."

"Don't mention it." He stroked a hand over her hair, let his fingers drift into it, through it. "You're taking on a lot, letting her and the kids stay with you. I can take them out to the farm. We've got plenty of room."

"She needs a woman, Rafe, not a bunch of men— however well-intentioned. Devin will find him, won't he? And take care of it?"

"You can count on it."

Satisfied, she picked up her own tea. "Then I will, and so should you." Now that the step had been taken, she eyed him over her cup. "You must have come by for a reason."

"I wanted to look at you for a while." Her bland gaze

had his lips curving. "And I figured to go over some of the wall treatments—and the parlor furniture. I want to complete that one room, give me a feel for the rest."

"That's a nice idea. I—" She broke off at the sound of movement and voices from the shop. "I've got customers. Everything's here—the paint samples and fabrics, itemized lists of furnishings."

"I picked up some samples of my own."

"Oh, well, then…" She crossed to the desk, booted up her computer. "I have a room-by-room rundown here. Why don't you go over it? Several of the pieces I've suggested are here. You can take a look at them when you've finished here."

"All right."

Thirty minutes later, flush with three sales, Regan stepped back into the office. He looked so big, she thought, so…male, sitting at her lovely little Chippendale desk. She could smell him—wood dust, soot, oil.

His boots were scarred, his shirt was ripped at the shoulder. There were traces of plaster or drywall dust in his hair.

She thought he was the most magnificent animal she had ever seen. And she wanted him with a kind of primal, mindless lust.

Whoa! To steady herself, she pressed a hand to her jumpy stomach, took three deep breaths.

"Well, what do you think?"

"You're an efficient woman, Regan." Without turning, he flipped open a file with printouts of her lists. "It doesn't look like you've missed a trick."

Flattered, she walked over to look over his shoulder. "I'm sure we'll need to adjust, add a few details after we see one of the rooms completed."

"I've already made some adjustments."

She straightened again. "Oh, really?"

"This color's out." Briskly he tapped the paint chip, then located the page on-screen where her colors were listed. "I ditched this pea green here for—what's it called? Yeah. Loden."

"The original color is accurate."

"It's ugly."

Yes, it was, but— "It's accurate," she insisted. "I researched very carefully. The one you've chosen is entirely too modern for the 1800s."

"Maybe. But it won't spoil anyone's appetite. Don't get your panties in a twist, darling." When her breath hissed out at that, he chuckled and turned around in the chair. "Listen, you're doing a hell of a job here. I have to admit, I didn't expect this much detail, certainly not so fast. You've got a real feel for it."

She didn't care to be placated. "You hired me to help you reconstruct a particular era, and that's what I'm doing. It was your choice to make the house look the way it did in the past."

"And it's my choice to make adjustments. We've got to make some room here for aesthetics and modern taste. I've had a look at your place upstairs, Regan. It's a little too much on the female side for me—"

"Fortunately, that's hardly the issue here," she told him, stiffening all over again.

"And so neat a man'd be afraid to put his feet up," Rafe continued smoothly. "But you've got taste. I'm just asking you to use it, along with research and accuracy."

"It seems to me we're talking about your taste. If you're going to change the guidelines, at least make them clear."

"Are you always so rigid, or is it just with me?"

She refused to stoop to answering such an insulting question. "You asked for accuracy. I don't care to have rules changed in midstream."

Considering, Rafe picked up the paint chip that had

started the ball rolling. "One question. Do you like this color?"

"That's not the point—"

"Simple question. Do you like it?"

Her breath whistled between her teeth. "Of course not. It's hideous."

"There you go. Guidelines are, if you don't like it, it doesn't fly."

"I can't take the responsibility."

"I'm paying you to take it." Since that settled the matter as far as he was concerned, he turned back to the screen, and scanned down the displays. "You got this what-do-you-call-it in stock, right? Isn't that what this I.S. stands for?"

"Yes. The double chairback settee." Her heart dropped to her feet. She'd bought it the week before at auction, with his parlor in mind. If he rejected it, her books were going straight into the red. "It's in the shop," she continued, keeping her voice coolly professional. "I've put a hold on it."

"So, let's take a look. I want to see this fire-screen and these tables."

"You're the boss," she muttered under her breath, and led the way.

Her nerves strained as she stopped by the settee. It was a gorgeous piece, and it had had a price to match. However much she coveted it, she would never have made the bid if she hadn't had a customer in the wings.

Now, she thought of that customer—the scarred boots, the ripped shirt, the potent aura of man. What had she been thinking of, she wondered frantically, imagining Rafe MacKade approving of an elegant, curvy, and decidedly feminine piece such as this?

"Ah, it's walnut…" she began, running a suddenly icy hand over the carved arm. "Around 1850. It's been reupholstered, of course, but the material is very much in keeping with the era. You can see the double-shaped backs are centered by a circular upholstered panel. The workmanship is first-rate, and the seat is surprisingly comfortable."

He grunted and crouched down to peer under the seat. "Pricey little thing."

"It's sixty-nine inches wide, and well worth the expense."

"Okay."

She blinked. "Okay?"

"Yeah. If I stay on schedule, I should have the parlor ready by the weekend. I could take delivery on this by

Monday, unless I tell you different." He glanced up at her. "That suit you?"

"Yes." She realized she'd lost all feeling below the knees. "Of course."

"C.O.D. all right? I don't have my checkbook on me."

"That'll be fine."

"Let's see the Pembroke table."

"The Pembroke table." She looked dizzily around the shop. "Over here."

He straightened, holding back a grin. He wondered if she had any idea that, for a few minutes there, she'd been clear as glass. He doubted it.

"What's this?"

Distracted, she stopped. "Oh, that's a display table. Satinwood and mahogany."

"I like it."

"You like it," she repeated.

"It'd look good in the parlor, wouldn't it?"

"Yes, I had it down as a possibility."

"Send it over with the couch thing. Is this the Pembroke here?"

All she could do was nod weakly. When he left, an hour later, she was still nodding.

* * *

Rafe headed straight to the sheriff's office. He'd have to put in a couple of hours overtime on the job, but he wasn't leaving town until he knew Joe Dolin was in a cage.

When he stepped inside, he found Devin tilted back in his chair, his feet propped on his battered metal desk. Devin's uniform consisted of a cotton shirt, faded jeans and boots worn down at the heel. His only concession to his position was the star on his chest.

He was reading a dog-eared copy of *The Grapes of Wrath.*

"And you're responsible for law and order in this town."

In his slow, deliberate way, Devin marked his place and set the book aside. "That's what they tell me. Always got a cell waiting for you."

"If you've got Dolin in one, I wouldn't mind you putting me in with him for five minutes or so."

"He's back there."

With a nod, Rafe walked to the coffeemaker. "Have any trouble with him?"

Devin's lips curved in a lazy and wicked smile. "Just enough to make it fun. I'll have a cup of that."

"How long can you keep him in there?"

"That's not up to me."

Devin reached out for the chipped mug Rafe offered. Since he insisted on making the coffee himself, it was the MacKade brew. Hot, strong and black as night.

"We'll transfer him to Hagerstown," Devin went on. "He'll get himself a public defender. If Cassie doesn't back down, he'll have his day in court."

Rafe sat on the corner of the cluttered desk. "You think she'll back down?"

Fighting frustration, Devin shrugged. "This is the closest she's ever come to doing anything about things. The son of a bitch has been pounding on her for years. Probably started on her on their wedding night. She can't weigh more than a hundred pounds. Got bones like a bird." His usually calm eyes went molten. "She's got bruises around her throat where he choked her."

"I didn't see that."

"I got pictures."

After rubbing a hand over his face, Devin dropped his feet to the floor. Tussling with Joe, slapping cuffs on him, along with a few bruises—in the line of duty— hadn't taken the edge off.

"I had to take her statement, and pictures for evidence, and she sat there looking at me like she was getting beat up all over again. God knows how she'll handle it if she has to go to court and lay it all out."

Abruptly he pushed away from his desk, paced to the window, where he could look out on the town. He'd given his word to serve the town, protect its citizens. Not to relieve his own bitter frustrations by pummeling one of them into the ground.

"I gave her the standard lines," he continued. "Therapy, counseling, shelters. And I put just enough pressure on when she started to waffle, so she'd sign the complaint. She just sat there crying, and I felt like scum."

Rafe studied his coffee, frowned. "You still have a thing for her, Dev?"

"That was high school," Devin snapped. With an effort, he uncurled his fist, turned back to his brother.

They might have been twins, with barely a year separating them. The same bold, dark looks, rangy build. Only Devin's eyes were cooler, more like moss than jade. And the scars he carried were on his heart.

"Sure I care about her," he said, calm again. "Hell, Rafe, we've known her all our lives. I've hated watching what he's been doing to her, not being able to stop it. Every time I got called out to their place, every time she had a fresh bruise, she'd just say it was an accident."

"Not this time."

"No, not this time. I sent my deputy with her to get the kids, whatever stuff she needs."

"You know she's going to stay with Regan Bishop."

"She told me." He drained his coffee, went back for more. "Well, she's taken the first step. It's probably the hardest."

Since there was nothing more he could do, Devin sat behind his desk again and put the matter in the corner of his mind. "Speaking of Regan Bishop, word is you've been sniffing around her."

"There a law against it?"

"If there is, it wouldn't be one you haven't broken before." Devin rose again, rooted through the side drawer of his deputy's desk. He confiscated two candy bars, tossed one to Rafe. "She's not your usual type."

"I'm upgrading my taste."

"'Bout time." Devin bit into chocolate. "Serious?"

"Getting a woman into bed's always serious, bro."

Mumbling an agreement over candy, Devin kicked back again. "So is that all there is?"

"I don't know. But I've got a feeling it'll be a hell of a start." He glanced over and grinned as Regan came through the door.

She stopped short, as any woman might when faced with two gorgeous men smiling at her. "I'm sorry. I'm interrupting."

"No, ma'am." All quiet country charm, Devin unfolded himself and stood. "It's always a pleasure to see you."

Angling his head, Rafe put a hand on Regan's shoulder. "Dibs," he said in a mild warning.

"Excuse me?" Regan stepped back and gaped. "I beg your pardon, but did you just say 'Dibs'?"

"Yeah." Rafe bit off candy, offered her the rest of the bar. When she smacked his hand away, he only shrugged and ate it himself.

"Of all the ridiculous, outrageous— You're a grown man, and you're standing there eating candy and saying 'Dibs' as if I were the last ice-cream bar in the freezer."

"The way I grew up, it was real important to stake your claim quick." To prove it, he cupped her elbows, lifted her to her toes and kissed her long and hard. "Gotta go," he said, releasing her just as arrogantly. "See you, Dev."

"Yeah." Too wise to let the laugh loose, Devin cleared his throat. Seconds passed, and Regan continued to stare at the door Rafe had slammed at his back. "You want me to go after him, haul him into the back room?"

"Have you got a rubber hose back there?"

"Afraid not. But I broke his finger once, when we were kids. I could probably do it again."

"Never mind." She shook herself. She'd deal with Rafe later, personally. "I came here to see if you'd arrested Joe Dolin."

"So did Rafe."

"I should have known he would."

"Want some coffee, Regan?"

"No, I can't stay. I just came to see if you had, and to ask, since Cassie and the children are going to be staying with me, if there are any precautions I should take."

Quietly he measured her. He'd known her casually for three years, admired her looks, enjoyed a few conversations with her at the café or on the street. Now he saw what had attracted his brother. Spine, good sense, compassion.

He wondered if Rafe understood the difference the combination could make in his life.

"Why don't you sit down," he told her. "We'll go over some things."

Chapter 5

On Monday morning, Regan was up early, a song on her lips. In a few hours, the first furnishings would be delivered to the house on the hill. With her payment deposited, she would dash to an auction in Pennsylvania scheduled for that afternoon.

It would be well worth closing the shop for the day.

She put the coffee on, popped bread into the toaster. Then turned and nearly jumped out of her slippers.

"Oh, Connor." Laughing, she pressed a hand to her speeding heart. "You scared me."

"I'm sorry." The boy was thin, pale, with big eyes the color of shadows. His mother's eyes, Regan thought as she smiled at him.

"It's okay. I didn't know anyone was up. It's early, even for a school day. Want some breakfast?"

"No, thank you."

She bit back a sigh. No eight-year-old boy should be so apologetically polite. She lifted a brow and took out a box of the cereal she'd learned was his favorite. With a wink, she gave it a shake.

"How about joining me for a bowl?"

He smiled then, so sweetly shy it broke her heart. "I guess if you're having some."

"Why don't you get the milk out, put it on the table?" Because it hurt to see how carefully, how deliberately, he performed the simple chore, she made her voice bright. "I heard on the radio we're in for some more snow. Maybe a big one."

She carried out bowls and spoons, set them down. When she lifted a hand to brush it over his tousled hair, he went very still. Cursing Joe Dolin, she kept the smile on her face. "I bet they close school tomorrow."

"I like school," he said then bit his lip.

"I always did, too." Brisk and determinedly cheerful, she breezed into the kitchen again for her coffee. "I never minded a day off now and again, but I really liked school. What's your favorite subject?"

"English class. I like to write things."

"Really? What kind of things?"

"Stories." He hunched his shoulders, looking down. "Just stupid stuff."

"I bet it's not." She could only hope she wasn't making a mistake, moving into territory best left to the experts. But her heart simply moved her hand. She cupped it under Connor's chin and lifted it gently as she sat beside him. "You should be proud. I know your mother's proud of you. She told me you won a prize in your English class for a story you wrote."

"She did?" He was torn between wanting to smile and wanting to let his head drop again. But Regan had her hand on his face. It felt good there, warm. The tears were in his eyes before he could stop them. "She cries at night."

"I know, baby."

"He was always hitting her. I knew it. I could hear them. But I never did anything to stop it. I never did anything to help her."

"You're not to blame." Letting instinct rule, she lifted him onto her lap, cuddling him close. "You're not to blame, Connor. And there was nothing you could have done. But now you and your mother and your little sister are safe. You're all going to look after each other."

"I hate him."

"Shh…" Jolted by how such fierceness could spurt from someone so small, so young, Regan pressed her lips to his hair and rocked.

In the hallway, Cassie stepped back. Torn in a dozen different directions, she swayed there a moment, a hand over her mouth. Then she went back into the little spare bedroom to wake her daughter for school.

Regan arrived at the Barlow place just ahead of the van and movers she'd hired. The cheerful noise of construction blasted her the minute she opened the door. Nothing could have lifted her mood higher.

The hallway was draped with tarps and drop cloths. But the spiderwebs and the mustiness were gone. The dust that lay now was fresh, and somehow clean.

She supposed it was a kind of exorcism. Amused by the thought, she studied the stairway. As a kind of test, she walked toward it, started up.

The cold slapped her like a fist, sending her back two steps. She stood, one hand gripping the rail, the other pressed to her stomach as she struggled to get back the breath the icy air had stolen.

"You've got guts," Rafe murmured from behind her.

Though her eyes were still wide in shock, she looked down and met his levelly. "I wondered if it had just been my imagination. How do the laborers go up and down these steps without—?"

"Not everyone feels it. I'd say the ones who do grit their teeth and think about their paycheck." He walked up the steps to take her hand. "How about you?"

"I'd never have believed it if I hadn't experienced it." Without protest, she let him lead her down to the main level. "It should make for some interesting breakfast conversation among the guests, once you're open."

"Darling, I'm counting on it. Give me your coat. We've got the heat for this part of the house up and running." He slipped her coat off himself. "It's on low, but it takes the edge off."

"You're telling me." Pleased that it seemed warm enough to make shivering unnecessary, she flipped back her hair. "What's going on upstairs?"

"A little bit of everything. I'm putting in an extra bath. I want you to dig up one of those claw-foot tubs, a pedestal sink. Reproductions'll do, if you don't have any luck finding originals."

"Give me a few days. Well." She rubbed her hands together, not from cold, but nerves. "Are you going to show me, or do I have to beg?"

"I'm going to show you." He'd been itching to, looking out the window every five minutes to watch for her. But now that she was here, he was nervous. He'd slaved for more than a week, twelve-and fourteen-hour days, to make that one room, that one spot, that one step, perfect.

"I think the paint turned out." Rather than reach for her hand, he tucked his in his pockets and walked into the parlor ahead of her. "It's a nice contrast with the trim and the floor, I think. Had a little trouble with the windows, but I just had to diddle with the framing."

She didn't speak. For a moment, she merely stood in the doorway. Then, quietly, her boots clicking on the floor, she stepped inside.

It gleamed. The tall, elegant windows, with their graceful arches sent sun streaming over the newly polished floor of lovely old pine. The walls were a deep, warm blue against creamy carved trim in the most delicate of ivories.

He'd turned the window seat into a charming alcove, scrubbed the marble on the fireplace until it shone like glass. The molding along the ceiling bloomed with delicately carved florets that had been smothered and choked by the grime of decades.

"It needs furniture, drapes, and that mirror you picked out for over the mantel." He wished she would say something, anything. "I have to replace the pocket doors, yet." Scowling, he jammed his hands deeper into his pocket. "Well, what's the problem? Did I miss some vital, authentic detail?"

"It's absolutely wonderful." Enchanted, she ran a finger down the glossy trim of a window. "Absolutely perfect. I didn't realize you were this good." With a quick laugh, she glanced back at him. "That wasn't meant as an insult."

"It wasn't taken as one. I was pretty surprised myself, the first time I realized I had a talent for putting something together."

"It's more than that. It's bringing something to life. You must be proud."

He was, he realized, moved, and just a little embarrassed. "It's a job. Hammer and nails and a good eye."

She angled her head, and he watched the sun beam

through the window and glow golden on her hair. His mouth watered, then went bone dry.

"You're the last man I'd expect to be modest about anything. You must have killed yourself to get so much accomplished in so little time."

"It was mostly cosmetic in here."

"You've done something," she murmured, and looked around, turning a slow, graceful circle. "You've really done something."

Before he could comment, she was on her hands and knees, running her hands over the floor.

"It's like glass." She all but crooned over the golden planks. "Oh, look at the grain in this wood! What did you use? How many coats?" When he didn't answer, she tossed her head and sat back on her heels. The dazzled smile faded when he only stared at her. "What is it? What's wrong?"

"Stand up."

His voice was raw. As she rose to her feet, he kept his distance. He didn't dare touch her now. If he did, he'd simply never be able to stop.

"You look right in here. You should see yourself, how right you look. You're as polished and perfect as this room. I want you so much I can't see anything else but you."

Her heart did a long, unsteady cartwheel in her chest. "You're going to make me stutter again, Rafe." She had to make a conscious effort to pump air in and out of her lungs.

"How long are you going to make me wait?" he demanded. "We're not kids. We know what we feel and what we want."

"That's exactly the point. We're not kids, and we should be adult enough to be sensible."

"Sensible's for old lady's shoes. Sex may have to be responsible, but it sure as hell doesn't have to be sensible."

The thought of wicked, completely insensible sex with him numbed every nerve ending in her body. "I don't know how to handle you. I don't know how to handle the way you make me feel. I'm usually good at handling things. I guess we need to talk about this."

"I guess you need to. I just said what I needed to say." Unbelievably frustrated, irrationally angry at his own helpless response to her, he turned to the window. "Your truck's here. I've got work upstairs. Put the stuff wherever the hell you want it."

"Rafe—"

He stopped her, froze her before her hand could reach his arm. "You wouldn't want to touch me right now." His voice was quiet, very controlled. "It'd be a mistake. You don't like to make them."

"That's not fair."

"What the hell makes you think I'm fair?" His eyes slashed her to ribbons. "Ask anybody who knows me. Your check's on the mantel."

With her own temper sizzling, she stomped into the hall after him. "MacKade."

He stopped on the steps, turned back. "Yeah?"

"I'm not interested in what anyone else thinks or says. If I were, you'd never have gotten within three feet of me."

She glanced up as an interested laborer poked his head into the stairway. "Beat it," she snapped, and had Rafe's lips twitching reluctantly. "I make up my own mind, in my own time," she continued and turned on her heel to open the front door for the movers. "*You* ask anybody."

When she looked back, he was gone, like one of his ghosts.

Nearly blew it, Rafe thought later. He wasn't entirely sure why he'd reacted that way. Anger and demands weren't his usual style with women. Maybe that, he mused as he troweled drywall compound on a seam, was the problem.

Women had always come easily.

He liked them, always had. The way they looked, thought, smelled, spoke. Soft, warm, fragrant, they were one of the more interesting aspects of life. Frowning, he slapped on more compound, smoothed it.

Women were important. He enjoyed cultivating them, the companionship they offered. And the sex, he acknowledged with a thin smile, he enjoyed that, too.

Hell, he was human.

Houses were important, he reflected, coating another seam of drywall. Repairing them was satisfying, using your own hands and sweat to turn them into something that lasted. And the money that came from the end result was satisfying, too.

A man had to eat.

But there'd never been a single house that was specifically important, as this one had come to be.

And there'd never been a single woman who was specifically important, as Regan had now become.

And he calculated that she would slice him into

dog meat if she knew he was comparing her to stone and wood.

He doubted she would understand that it was the first time in his life he'd ever focused on something, and someone, so entirely.

The house had haunted him for a lifetime. He hadn't set eyes on her a month before. Yet they were both in his blood. He hadn't been exaggerating when he told her that he couldn't see anything but her. She was haunting him, just as the restless ghosts haunted these rooms and hallways.

Seeing her there that morning had turned him on his head, set his hormones raging, and he'd fumbled. He supposed he could make up ground. But this was the first time he could remember being tackled by emotion—emotion double-teamed with desire—and he wasn't at all sure of his moves.

Back off, MacKade, he told himself, and scooped more compound out of the bucket. She wants room, give her room. It wasn't as though he didn't have time—or as though she were some sort of life-altering encounter. Maybe she was unique, maybe she was more intriguing than he'd counted on. But she was still just a woman.

He heard the weeping, felt the stir of chilled air. With barely a hesitation, he leveled his seam.

"Yeah, yeah, I hear you," he muttered. "You might as well get used to company, 'cause I'm not going anywhere."

A door slammed. It amused him now, these endless little dramas. Footsteps and creaks, whispers and weeping. It was almost as though he were part of it all. A caretaker, he decided. Making the house livable for those who could never leave.

He thought it was too bad none of the permanent residents ever made an appearance. It would be quite an experience to see, as well as hear. An involuntary shudder worked up his back, as if fingers had trailed along his spine.

And feel, he thought.

Footsteps echoed down the hall outside as he moved to the next sheet of drywall. To his surprise and curiosity, they stopped just outside the door. He watched the knob turn, just as the work lamp behind him went out, plunging the room into darkness.

He'd have suffered torments from hell before admitting that his heart skipped several beats. To cover the lapse, he muttered oaths under his breath, rubbed his suddenly damp palms on his spattered jeans. From memory, he fumbled his way toward the door. It swung open fast and caught him full in the face.

He wasn't muttering oaths now, but spewing them. Stars were revolving in front of his eyes. And, with disgust, he felt blood trickle from his nose.

He heard the hoarse scream, saw the ghostly figure in the shadows of the hall, and didn't hesitate. Pain and fury had him shooting forward like a bullet. Ghost or not, anything that gave him a bloody nose was going to pay.

It took him several furious seconds to realize he had warm flesh wriggling in his arms, and little more to recognize the scent.

She was haunting him all right, he thought bitterly.

"What the hell are you doing?"

"Rafe?" Her voice squeaked out. In the dark, she threw up her arms, one flailing hand catching him sharply on the chin before she managed the whole-hearted embrace. "Oh, my God, you scared me to death. I thought— I don't know. I heard... I came up. Oh, it's you."

"What's left of me." Swearing, he set her firmly aside. There was enough light from the lamp hooked at the top of the stairs for him to see her pale face and huge eyes. "What are you doing here?"

"I picked up some things at auction and thought I'd put them— You're bleeding."

"No kidding." Scowling at her, he swiped a hand under his nose. "I don't think you broke it again. Quite."

"I—" She rubbed a hand over her heart to make sure it hadn't exploded from her chest. "Did I hit you with the door? I'm sorry. Here." She dug in the pocket of her jacket and found a tissue. "I'm really sorry," she repeated, and began to dab at the blood herself. "I was just…" Helpless, she tried to disguise a laugh as a hiccup. "I didn't realize." She gave up, wrapped her arms around her aching stomach, and slid to the floor.

"It's a real laugh riot."

"I'm sorry. I can't stop. I thought—I don't know what I thought. I heard them, or it, or whatever. I just had to come up and see, well, if I could see. Then you came barreling out."

"You're lucky I didn't punch you," he said, with relish.

"I know. I know."

His eyes narrowed as he watched her fold with mirth. "I still could."

"Oh, help me up." Still chuckling, she wiped at her eyes. "Let's get some ice on that nose."

"I can take care of it myself." But he took hold of her wrist and hauled her, none too gently, to her feet.

"Did I scare you?" She tried to keep her voice meek and apologetic as she followed him to the stairs.

"Get real."

"But you heard—you heard it, didn't you?" She braced, held her breath as they passed through the cold spot.

"Sure, I heard it. Goes on every night. A couple times during the day."

"And it doesn't...bother you?"

It boosted his ego to be able to flick a disdainful glance over his shoulder. "Why should it bother me? It's their house, too."

"I suppose." She looked around the kitchen. It was all but bare, and still grimy. There was a small, dented refrigerator, a stove that was down to two working burners, and an old door propped on sawhorses that served as a table. Rafe went directly to the pitted cast-iron sink and ran cold water. "Do you have a clean rag?"

In lieu of an answer, he bent over and scooped icy water onto his face. Adopting a shamed pose, Regan folded her hands.

"I'm really terribly sorry, Rafe. Does it hurt?"

"Yes."

He snatched up a frayed towel and dried his face. Without another word, he strode to the refrigerator and pulled out a beer.

"It's stopped bleeding."

He twisted off the top, tossed it aside, then downed a third of the bottle. Regan decided that, under the circumstances, she could try again.

"I didn't see your car. That's why I didn't think anyone was here."

"Devin dropped me off." He decided that, under the circumstances, he could give her a break. "I've been putting in some extra time at night, camping out here. We're supposed to get hit with a snowstorm tonight, so it didn't make any sense to have the car. I can walk into town if I need to."

"Oh. Well. That explains it."

"Want a beer?"

"No thanks, I don't drink beer."

"Fresh out of champagne."

"Well, then, I really should be getting back. Actually, it's already starting to snow." Feeling awkward now, she pushed at her hair. "Ah, there were these candlesticks, and a really wonderful set of fire irons I bought today. I just wanted to bring them by, see how they looked."

He lifted the beer again, watching her. "So, how do they look?"

"I don't know. I set everything down in the hall when I came in and heard the, ah, evening performance."

"You decided to go ghost hunting instead of decorating."

"Looks that way. Well, why don't I set them up now, before I take off?"

Taking the beer along, he went with her. "I guess you've cooled off since this morning."

"Not exactly." She spared him a brief look as she headed to the main hall. "Though giving you a bloody nose, even inadvertently, was satisfying. You acted like a jerk."

His eyes narrowed as she picked up the box she'd left in the hall and sailed into the parlor. "I was giving it to you straight. Some women appreciate honesty."

"Some women like jerks." She set the box on a drum table she'd had the movers place at the window. "I don't. I like simplicity, manners, tact. Which, of course, you're completely without." Then she turned, and smiled. "But I think, under the circumstances, a truce is in order. Who broke your nose before?"

"Jared, when we were kids and fighting in the hay-loft. He got lucky."

"Hmm..." She supposed she would never under-stand why brotherly affection meant bloody noses to the MacKades. "So this is where you're camping out." She gestured toward the sleeping bag tossed in front of the fire.

"It's the warmest room in the house right now. And the cleanest. What circumstances equal a truce?"

"Don't set that bottle down without a coaster." Heaving a sigh, she walked over, took one from the silver-plated basket and offered it. "You can't treat antiques like..."

"Furniture?" he finished, but he used the coaster. "What circumstances, Regan?"

"Our ongoing business relationship, for one." Be-cause her fingers were tense again, she busied them by unbuttoning her coat as she walked back to the window. "We're both trying to accomplish the same thing with this house, so it doesn't make sense to be at odds. These are nice, aren't they?" She took the fire irons from the box, stroked a finger over the curved handle of the coal shovel. "They could use some polish."

"It ought to work better than the crowbar I've been using." Tucking his thumbs in his pockets, he watched her carry the irons to the fire, set them carefully and individually in their stand on the stone hearth.

"Whatever you used, it's a nice fire." Torn between courage and doubt, she stared at the flames. "I'm still looking for the right screen. This one doesn't really suit. It would be better in one of the rooms upstairs. I imagine you'll have them all working. The fireplaces."

"Eventually."

He'd only known her for a few weeks, he realized. How could he be so sure she was arguing with herself? With the firelight flickering over her, her back so straight, that sweep of hair curtaining half her face, she looked relaxed, confident, perfectly at ease. Maybe it was the way she had her fingers linked together, or the way she wasn't looking at him. But he was certain some small inner war was being waged.

"Why are you here, Regan?"

"I told you." Dragging her fingers apart, she went back to the box. "I have some other stuff from the auction in my car, but you're not ready for it. But these…" With care, she unwrapped heavy crystal candlesticks. "I could see them in here, right on this table. You'll want flowers for this vase. Even in the winter."

She fussed with the arrangement, placing the candlesticks just so on one side of the Doulton vase she'd already sold him.

"Tulips would be lovely, when you can get them," she continued, carefully unwrapping the two white tapers she'd brought along. "But mums would do, and roses, of course." She put a smile on her face again and turned. "There, what do you think?"

Saying nothing, he took a box of wooden matches from the mantel and walked over to light the tapers. And watched her over the delicate twin flames. "They work."

"I meant the whole effect, the room." It was a good excuse to move away from him, wandering the space, running a finger along the curved back of the settee.

"It's perfect. I didn't expect any less from you."

"I'm not perfect." The words burst out of her, unexpected on both sides. "You make me nervous when you say so. I was always expected to be perfect, and I'm just not. I'm not carefully arranged, like this room, with every piece in place, no matter how much I want to be. I'm a mess." She dragged nervous fingers through her hair. "And I wasn't, before. I wasn't. No, stay over there." She backed up quickly when he stepped forward. "Just stay over there."

Frustrated, she waved her hands to ward him off, then paced. "You scared me this morning. You made me angry, but more, you scared me."

It wasn't easy for Rafe to keep his hands to himself. "How?"

"Because no one's ever wanted me the way you do. I know you do." She stopped, rubbing her hands over her arms. "You look at me as though you already know how it's going to be with us. And I have no control over it."

"I figured I was giving you control, laying it out for you."

"No. No," she repeated, flinging up her arms. "I don't have any control over the way I'm feeling. You have to know that. You know exactly the way you affect people."

"We're not talking about people."

"You know exactly the way you affect *me*." She almost shouted it before she fisted her hands and fought for composure. "You know I want you. Why wouldn't I? It's just as you said, we're adults who know what we want. And the more I backpedal, the more stupid I feel."

His eyes were shadowed in the shifting light. "You're going to stand there and say these things to me and expect me to do nothing about it?"

"I expect to be able to make a sane and rational decision. I don't expect my glands to overwhelm my brain." She blew out a breath. "Then I look at you and I want to rip your clothes off."

He had to laugh. It was the safest way to defuse the bomb ticking inside of him. "Don't expect me to stop you." When he stepped forward, she jumped back like a spring. "Just the beer," he muttered, lifting the bottle. "I need it." He took a long, deep gulp, but it didn't do much to put out the fire. "So, what have we got here, Regan? Two unattached, healthy adults who want pretty much the same thing from each other."

"Who barely know each other," she added. "Who've barely scratched the surface of any sort of relationship.

Who should have more sense than to jump into sex as if it was a swimming pool."

"I never bother testing the water."

"I do. An inch at a time." Ordering herself to be calm, she linked her hands again. "It's important to me to know exactly what I'm getting into, exactly where I'm going."

"No detours?"

"No. When I plan something, I stick to it. That works for me." She was calmer now, she told herself. Rational now. "I had a lot of time to think, driving to Pennsylvania and back. We need to slow down, take a look at the whole picture."

If she was calm, why couldn't she stop fiddling with her blazer, twisting her rings?

"It's like this house," she continued quickly. "You've finished one room, and it's beautiful, it's wonderful. But you didn't start this project without a complete plan in mind for the rest of it. I think intimacy should certainly be as carefully thought out as the renovation of a house."

"Makes sense."

"Good." She drew in a breath, released it. "So, we'll take a few steps back, get a clearer view of things."

Her hand was still unsteady when she reached for her coat. "That's the sensible, the responsible route to take."

"Yeah." He set down his beer. "Regan?"

She gripped her coat like a lifeline. "Yes."

"Stay."

Her fingers went numb. Her breath came out in a long, shuddering sigh. "I thought you'd never ask."

With a jittery laugh, she threw herself into his arms.

Chapter 6

"This is crazy." Already breathless, she curled her fingers into his hair to drag his mouth to hers. Everything in her strained into the kiss, the heat of it, the danger, the promise. "I wasn't going to do this."

"That's okay." He dragged his lips from hers to race over her face. "I'll do it."

"I'd thought it all through." When her knees trembled, she gave a quick, helpless laugh. "I had. Everything I just said made perfect sense. This is just chemistry. It's just superficial attraction."

"Yeah." In one fluid movement, he yanked her blazer down her shoulders, locking her arms, trapping her body to his. Her gasp of alarm stirred his blood. The huge, wary eyes tightened his loins. "Stop thinking."

A smile curved his lips as he tugged the bunched material, pressing her against him. He watched her eyes glaze, heard the ragged moan when his mouth fed on hers. Then his lips rushed down over the line of her throat. It was as smooth, as scented, as he'd imagined it. So he feasted.

Her hands clutched at his hips, her head falling back to offer him whatever he chose to take. All the while the heat coursed through her painfully, forcing her breath out in harsh, ragged moans.

With a jerk, he freed her arms. Before she could reach out, his hands, his wide, clever hands, streaked under her sweater to mold, to possess.

Flesh and lace, curves and shudders. He found everything he wanted, and wanted more. His mouth continued its relentless assault, while his fingers tortured her skin, and her skin tortured him.

With a flick of his wrist, he unsnapped her trousers, then skimmed the tips of his fingers along her quivering belly, under the edge of more lace. She moved against him, pressed urgently against him, her teeth scraping along his neck in greedy bites.

He could take her now, fast and hot, where they stood. The speed would release this terrible pressure that burned inside him.

But he wanted more.

He dragged the sweater over her head, tossed it aside and filled his palms with her breasts. The lace covering was smooth, delicate, and the flesh beneath already flushed and warm with desire. Ruthlessly controlling the pounding need to rush, Rafe watched her face, the flicker of light and shadow over it, while he rubbed his work-roughened thumbs over the points of her breasts.

"I've imagined you like this."

"I know."

His lips curved again, and his eyes were focused keenly on hers when he nudged a slim strap down her shoulder. "I don't think you've imagined what I've thought of doing to you. I don't think you could. So I'm going to show you."

His eyes stayed on hers, watching, measuring, as he skimmed a finger along the valley between her breasts, up over the curve, then back to flick open the center clasp.

So he saw that lovely sky blue gaze darken with

the storm he set off inside her. And he felt it quake, in both of them.

Her breath caught in her throat when he jerked her off her feet and set his hungry mouth to work. Shocked, she arched back, her hands fumbling in his hair, over his shoulders, tugging desperately at his shirt. His teeth nipped into her, just short of savage, just short of pain. His tongue tormented, and aroused needs too violent to bear.

Wild, frantic, she clawed at him. Even as she felt herself falling, she tore and ripped at his shirt. She was on her back, on the thin cushion of the sleeping bag, and bucking desperately beneath him.

Finally she tugged his shirt away, cursing when she found yet another layer separating them. She wanted flesh, craved it with a mindless hunger. The moment he'd dragged the thin undershirt aside, she sank her teeth into his shoulder.

"Touch me." Her words were raw and urgent. "I want your hands on me."

They were, everywhere at once. Her world became primitive, dangerously exciting, pumped full to bursting with unspeakable sensations. Each rough, impatient caress sent fresh shocks erupting, until her body was nothing but sweaty flesh over sparking nerves.

Beside her, the fire shot hissing embers against the screen. Inside her, flames leapt and burned.

She could see him through the haze that blurred her vision. The dark hair, the fierce eyes, the muscles that glistened with sweat in the dance of light. Her moan of protest when his mouth left hers turned to one of giddy pleasure as his lips streaked down over throat, over breasts and torso.

He levered back and, blind with need, she reared up, her arms circling possessively, her lips searching for each new taste.

His oath was brief and vicious. "Boots," he managed, fighting to pry hers off while his blood screamed. She was draped around him, that wonderful body sliding over his, her hands... Those incredible elegant hands.

Boots thudded where he heaved them aside, then, quick as a snake, turned to take her.

She was tangled around him, all long, silky limbs. He wanted her naked and writhing beneath him. He wanted to hear her scream his name and watch the jolts and shocks of pleasure glaze her eyes. Breath ragged, he dragged the slacks down her hips. In one reckless swipe, he tore the lace to shreds. Even as her gasp echoed off the walls, he shoved her back. And used his mouth.

The climax slammed into her, a bare-knuckled punch that knocked her senseless. Reeling from it, she sobbed out his name. And, shuddering, shuddering, hungered for more.

He gave her more. And took more. Each time she thought he would end it, must end it, he found some new way to batter her senses. There was only him, the taste, the feel, the smell of him. They rolled over the floor in a wild, glorious combat, her nails digging ruthlessly into his back, his mouth searing hers.

Nearly blinded by need, he gripped her hands, fingers vised. He thought his own breathing must tear his lungs apart. Her face was all he could see as he drove himself into her. Twin groans mixed. A log shattered thunderously in the grate.

They trembled, watching each other as they savored that timeless instant of mating.

Muscles straining, he lowered his head, covered her mouth. When the kiss was at its deepest, when her flavor filled him as intimately as he was filling her, they began to move together.

It was the cold that finally roused Regan. Though it seemed impossible, she thought she must have fallen asleep. As she struggled to orient herself, she discovered her back was against the cold, hard wood of the floor, pressed firmly against it by the weight of Rafe's body.

She looked around dazedly. Somehow or other, they'd gotten themselves several feet from the fire.

"You awake now?" Rafe's voice was thick, a little sleepy.

"I guess." She tried a deep breath, was relieved to find she could accomplish it. "I can't really tell."

He shifted his head, skimmed his lips over the curve of her breast. Her exhausted body quivered in response.

"I guess I can tell after all," she said.

"You're cold." He shifted, hauled her up and put her back on the sleeping bag. Wished, for her, that it was a feather bed. "Better?"

"Yeah." Not quite sure of her moves, she tugged a corner of the bag up to her chin. She'd never been so exposed, so completely naked, body and soul, before anyone. "I must have dozed off."

"Just a couple minutes." He grinned at her. He felt as though he'd climbed a mountain. And could climb ten more. "I'll put another log on."

Naked and easy, he rose to go to the woodbox. The scratches scoring his shoulders had Regan's mouth falling open. She'd done that. She'd actually… Good God. "I, ah, should go. Cassie'll be worried."

Rafe set the screen back in place. Without a word, he reached into the duffel bag beside the woodbox and took out a cell phone. "Call her."

"I…didn't realize you had a phone."

"It's a tool on a job like this." He handed it to her, then sat down beside her. "Call her," he repeated. "And stay."

She was sure there were reasons why she should go. But she dialed her own number, watching Rafe as the phone rang.

"Cassie, it's Regan. Yes, everything's fine. Snow?" Baffled for a moment, she pushed her hair away from her face. "Oh, yes, it's really coming down. That's why I'm calling. I got, um, involved, and I think…"

She trailed off as Rafe tugged the corner of the bag

out of her hand, as his fingers trailed down the curve of her breast.

"What?" She swallowed, then bit back a moan. His mouth had replaced his fingers. She slid bonelessly to her back. "Pennsylvania?" she murmured. "No, I'm not in Pennsylvania."

Rafe took the phone from her limp fingers. "She's with me. She's staying with me. No kidding? She'll call you tomorrow. Right."

He clicked the phone off, set it aside. "Cassie says we've got over a foot out there, the streets are a mess, and you should stay put."

"Oh." She closed her eyes, lifted her arms. "That's very sensible."

The candles had guttered out and the fire had burned to embers when she awoke. The house was so still, so quiet, she could hear her own heartbeat. The room was filled with shadows and darkness, but it was oddly peaceful. Perhaps the ghosts slept, she mused. Or perhaps she felt at ease with them because Rafe slept beside her.

She turned her head and studied his face in the dying firelight. Asleep or not, she mused, there was no innocent-little-boy look about him. All that power, and the potential for violence, were still there, carved into his face.

She knew he could be gentle, caring. She'd seen that in the way he was with Cassie. But as a lover, he was demanding, relentless and rough.

And, for the first time in her life, she'd been the same.

Now, with the quiet like a blanket over her, she found it hard to believe she had done what she'd done, had allowed him—wanted him—to do what he had done.

Her body ached from bruises, and she wondered if in the full light of day she would wince at the memory of how she'd come by them. Of how she'd ached and trembled and hungered under those big, hard hands.

Even more, of how she'd used her own.

Of how, she realized with a jolt, she wanted to use them now.

Taking a shallow breath, she eased out from under Rafe's possessive arm. She moved as quietly as she could, settled on slipping on his flannel shirt for covering. Buttoning it as she went, she padded toward the kitchen.

A cold drink of water, she told herself. A few moments to evaluate the situation.

At the sink, she filled a glass. As her eyes adjusted, she watched the drift of snow falling outside the window.

She didn't regret. That, she mused, would be foolish. Fate had placed an extraordinary lover in her path. The kind of man few women ever knew. She could, and would, be content with the physical thrill of it. She could, and would, prevent it, and him, from complicating her life.

They were both adults, as he had said. They both knew what they wanted. When the house was finished, he would probably grow restless and move on. Meanwhile they would enjoy each other. And when it was over, it would end with mutual understanding, and, she hoped, affection.

It would probably be wise to discuss those expectations, or the lack of them, before things went any further. But she found herself torn at the very idea of voicing them.

From the doorway, Rafe studied her, the way she stood, leaning a little on the counter, her eyes on the window. Her face reflected in it. His shirt skimmed her thighs, worn flannel against creamy skin.

It struck him, hard, that he'd never in his life seen anything more beautiful. He had the words to tell her; he was good with them. But he found there were none this time, none good enough to show how much she mattered.

So he chose easy ones, casual ones, and ignored the ache just looking at her had spreading around his heart.

"I like your dress, darling."

She jolted, nearly bobbled the glass before she turned. He'd tugged on jeans, but hadn't bothered to fasten them. Grinning, he leaned against the unframed doorway.

"It was handy," she said, matching his tone.

"That old shirt's never had it so good. Restless?"

"I was thirsty." But she set the glass down without taking so much as a sip. "I guess the quiet woke me. It's odd, don't you think, how quiet it is?"

"The snow always makes it quiet."

"No, I mean the house. It seems different. Settled."

"Even dead soldiers and unhappy women have to sleep sometime." He crossed the room to pick up the glass and drink himself. "It's almost dawn," he murmured. "My brothers and I spent the night here once when we were kids. I guess I told you that already."

"Jared rattling chains. And all of you telling ghost stories and smoking stolen cigarettes."

"You got it. I came into this room then, too. It was just about this time of day, but it was late summer. Everything was so green, and the woods were so dense and thick they made you wonder what was in them. There was a mist over the ground like a river. It was beautiful, and I thought—" He broke off, shrugged.

"No." She laid a hand on his arm. "Tell me."

"I thought I could hear the drums, slowly, the sounds of camps breaking to prepare for battle. I could smell the fear, the excitement, the dread. I thought I could hear the house waking around me, the whispers and creaks. I was petrified, paralyzed. If I could have moved, I'd have hauled my butt out of here. The guys would've rubbed my nose in it for years, but I'd have run like a rabbit if my legs had moved."

"You were just a boy."

"You've never been a boy, so you don't know that made it ten times worse. I'd gotten through the night, even gotten a kick out of it. And here it was morning, dawn breaking, and I stood here with my teeth chattering. When it passed, I just stood looking out this window. And I thought, no damn house is going to get the better of me. Nothing's going to get the better of me. I'll own this house before I'm finished."

He smiled then, set the glass down. "I don't know how many times I came back here, alone, after that. Waiting for something to happen, wishing it would, just so I could stand up to it. I crept through every room of this place at one time or another. I heard things, saw things, felt things. The night I left town, I promised myself I'd come back."

"Now you have it," she said quietly.

"Yeah." Faintly embarrassed, he looked down at her. "I never told anyone that."

"Then neither will I." She lifted a hand, touched his cheek. "Whatever your reasons, you're doing something important. This house has been neglected too long."

"Were you frightened, staying here through the night?"

"No. Not of the house."

His brow lifted. "Of me?"

"Yes. I'm frightened of you."

The humor faded from his eyes. "I was rough with you," he said carefully.

"I don't mean that." She turned away. Out of habit, she set a kettle on the stove, flicked on the burner. "I've never been the way I was last night, with anyone. So out of control. So…needy. I'm a little surprised when I think back and… Well." She let out a shaky breath, searched out a filter for the drip cone.

"Surprised? Or sorry?"

"Not sorry, Rafe." Making the effort, she turned back and met his eyes. "No, not sorry at all. Uneasy, because I know now exactly what you can do to me. I knew making love with you would be exciting. I didn't know it would be so shattering. Nothing about you is tidy or predictable. The way I like things to be."

"I want you now. That should be predictable."

"My heart jumps," she managed. "Literally, when you say things like that. But I do need things to be tidy." Opening the can of coffee, she deliberately measured out scoops. "I imagine your men will be coming along in an hour or so. This probably isn't the best time to talk this out."

"Nobody's coming today. There's better than two feet of snow out there, on top of what we already had."

"Oh." Her hand faltered, spilling ground coffee on the stove.

"We're snowbound for a while, darling. You can talk all you want."

"Well." After clearing her throat, she faced him again. "I just think it's best if we both understood things."

"What things?"

"Things." She bit the word off, furious at herself for hesitating. "Things that we didn't quite finish outlining last night. That what we're having is a mutual satisfying and physical affair, no strings, no entanglements, no…"

"Complications?"

"Yes." Relieved, she nodded. "Exactly."

Surprised to find himself annoyed with her coolheaded description—one that should have mirrored his own wishes—he scratched his head. "That's tidy enough. But if that means you're planning on seeing somebody else, it'll get messy when I break him in half."

"Oh, of all the ridiculous—"

"And cut off his—"

"Stop that." She blew out a heated breath. "I have

no intention of seeing someone else while we're involved, but if I—"

"Smarter to stop there," he said quietly. "Let's just say we have a mutually satisfying and exclusive physical relationship. That suit you?"

Calmer, she turned back to pour boiling water through the filter. "Yes, I can agree to that."

"You're a piece of work, Regan. You want the contract in triplicate?"

"I only want to make sure we expect the same things." She concentrated hard on covering the grounds with water, on being sure not to pour too much water, or too little. "We haven't taken time to really get to know each other. Now we're lovers. I don't want you to think I'm looking for any more than that."

"And if I'm looking for more?"

Her fingers whitened on the handle of the kettle. "Are you?"

He looked away from her, toward the window and the softly falling snow. "No."

She closed her eyes, telling herself it was relief she felt at his answer. Only relief. "Well, then there's no problem."

"No, everything's dandy." His voice was as cool and

detached as hers. "You don't want romance, saves me the trouble. You don't want promises, I don't have to lie. We want each other in bed." He reached for two mugs. "That keeps it simple."

"I want you in bed." Pleased with her casual tone, she took the mugs from him. "But if I didn't like who you are, we wouldn't have gotten there. I've wanted other men."

In a deceptively calm gesture, he flicked her hair behind her ear. "Now you're trying to make me mad."

The fact that he couldn't see how difficult it was for her to be so open, to keep things simple, made it easier. Oddly enough, this kind of openness seemed completely natural with him. "I'm trying to give you a compliment. I wouldn't have come here last night, hoping you'd be here, if I hadn't cared about you."

"You came to drop off candlesticks."

"You're an idiot." Amused at both of them, she poured coffee. She hadn't realized sexual frankness could be fun. "You didn't really buy that, did you?"

Intrigued, he took the mug she offered. "Yeah, I did."

She sipped, smiled. "Sucker."

"Maybe I don't like sneaky, aggressive women."

"Yes, you do. In fact, you're hoping I'll seduce you right now."

"Think so?"

"I know so. But I want my coffee first."

He watched her take another delicate sip. "Maybe I want my shirt back. You didn't ask if you could borrow it."

"Fine." With one hand, she undid the buttons. "Take it."

He nipped the coffee from her hand, set both mugs aside. Her smug smile had him scooping her off her feet. She was laughing and assaulting his ear as he carried her back down the hall. The front door swung open, letting in cold and blowing snow and a figure crusted with white.

Shane dragged off his cap and shook himself like a dog. "Hey." Casually he kicked the door closed. "Your car's buried to the wheel wells, Regan."

"Oh." With a fumbling hand, she clutched the shirt together and tried to mirror his easy tone. "We got a lot of snow."

"Over two feet." Unabashed, he grinned at his brother. "Figured you'd need someone to plow you out."

"Does it look like I want you to rescue me?" Disgusted, Rafe strode into the parlor and dumped Regan on the settee. "Stay right there."

"Rafe!" Futilely she tried to tug the hem of the shirt down over her legs. "For heaven's sake!"

"Right there," he repeated, and headed back into the hall.

"That coffee I smell?" Shane asked conversationally. "I could use some."

"Give me one reason why I shouldn't break your neck."

Shane took off his gloves, blew on his chilled fingers. "'Cause I rode over here in a blizzard to save yours." He leaned forward, but couldn't quite see into the parlor. "She's sure got legs."

"Where do you want to die?"

"Just an observation." His grin only widened, the MacKade dimple flashing. "Hey, who knew? I figured you were stuck here, without transportation. Alone. Then, when I saw her car, I thought maybe she needed a lift into town." Again he inched forward, hopeful. "Maybe I should ask her."

"One more step and they won't find your body till spring."

"If I win, can I keep her?" When Rafe snarled,

Shane erupted with laughter. "Don't hit me, I'm frozen. I'll break."

Muttering threats, Rafe grabbed Shane by the collar and dragged him down the hall. "Eyes front, MacKade." In the kitchen, he found a thermos, filled it with coffee. "Now beat it."

"I'm going." But Shane drank straight from the thermos. "The wind's a bitch." Grateful for the heat, he drank again. "Look, I didn't mean to horn in on your little love nest," he began, then stopped, lowered the thermos when he read quick fury in Rafe's eyes. "Hey, are you serious about her?"

"Mind your own damn business."

Shane whistled out a breath, screwed the top on the thermos. "You've always been my business. Regan's a real lady. I mean that."

"So?"

"So nothing." Embarrassed now, Shane shifted position. "I like her, always have. I thought about…" Realizing he'd taken a wrong turn, he pulled out his gloves again and whistled a cheerful tune.

"Thought about what?"

Cautious, Shane ran his tongue around his teeth. He really wanted to keep all of them. "Just what you think I thought. Hell, look at her. A man's bound to think." Agile, he evaded Rafe's lunging arm. "Think is all I did. I'm not going to fight you over thinking." In a gesture of peace, he threw up his hands. "What I'm saying is, it's great. You hit the jackpot."

Temper vanished. Rafe reached for the pot again. "We're sleeping together. That's all."

"You gotta start somewhere."

"She's different, Shane." He hadn't been able to admit it to himself, but it came easily brother to brother. "I haven't sorted it out, but she's different. She matters a lot."

"Everybody's got to take the big fall sometime." Shane slapped a hand on Rafe's bare shoulder. "Even you."

"I didn't say anything about falling," Rafe muttered. He knew the implications of that. Falling in love. Being in love.

"You didn't have to. Look, I'll plow the lane, just in case. You got any food around here?"

"Yeah, there's enough."

"I'll take off, then. It's supposed to let up by mid-morning. I have animals to tend to, so if you need something, try Devin first. I might be out."

"Thanks. Shane?" He turned, eyeing his brother.

"If you so much as glance in that parlor on your way out, I'll have to kill you."

"I already got a good look at her legs." Whistling cheerfully, Shane ambled down the hall. "See you, Regan." It cost him, but he kept his eyes averted on his way to the door.

The minute she heard it slam, Regan pressed her face on her updrawn knees. Stepping into the parlor, Rafe winced at her defensive posture, her trembling shoulders.

"Look, darling, I'm sorry. I should have locked the damn door." Gently he patted her shoulder and sat down beside her. "Shane doesn't mean to be an idiot. He was born that way. He doesn't mean any harm. Don't be upset."

She made a strangled sound, and when she lifted her face, it was wet with tears. Her laughter bubbled out like wine. "Can you imagine what we looked like, the three of us, in that hall?" She pressed her hand over her mouth and rocked. "The two of us half-naked, Shane looking like the abominable snowman."

"You think that's funny?"

"No, I think it's hysterical." Weak with laughter,

she collapsed against him. "The MacKade brothers. Oh, God, what have I gotten myself into?"

Delighted with her, he hauled her into his lap. "Give me back my shirt, darling, and I'll show you."

Chapter 7

Cozy in the sleeping bag, Regan dozed by the fire. It sizzled, logs crackling, and brushed heat over her face and her outflung arm. She sighed, cruising with the dream, shifting toward her lover.

Her dreams were nearly as erotic as the reality of the past hours, vivid enough to have her stirring, and yearning. When she reached out and found herself alone, she sighed again, in disappointment.

The fire was lively, so she knew Rafe had built it up once more before he left her. The room was quiet enough that she could hear the ticking of the mantel clock marking time. Evidence of the night's activities was all around her, in the hastily strewn clothes littering the floor, the torn bits of lace and the jumbled boots. And the evidence was within her as she stretched, feeling the warm glow of desire.

She wished he was there, so that he could stoke it as he had stoked the fire.

Still, it was a wonderful shock to realize she could lay claim to such a bottomless well of passion.

It had never been so before, she reflected, sitting up to exercise her stiff and sore muscles. Physical relationships had always been far down on her list of priorities. She wondered if, after her recent behavior, Rafe would be surprised to know that before him, she had considered herself hesitant, even a little shy, when it came to intimacy.

With a yawn, she reached for her sweater and pulled it over her head.

Knowing him, she decided, he'd just be smug.

It was a pity she couldn't blame her celibacy of the past few years for her wildfire response to him. It felt as though her libido had been nothing more than dry timber set to the torch the moment he put his hands on her. But using abstinence as the major reason for her response would be far from honest.

Whatever her life had been before, he'd changed it just by stepping into her path. It was certain she would never look at cozy nights by a fire in the same way again. It was doubtful she would look at anything in quite the same way again, she mused, now that she knew what she was capable of with the right...mate.

Just how, she wondered, did a woman go back to a quiet, settled life once she'd had a taste of Rafe MacKade? That was something she was going to have to deal with, one cautious day at a time.

At the moment, the only thing she wanted was to find him.

In her stocking feet, she began to wander the house. He could be anywhere, and the challenge of hunting him down, finding him busy with some chore—one she was determined to distract him from—amused her.

The chill of the bare floors seeped through and had her rubbing her hands together for a little warmth. But curiosity far overweighed a little discomfort.

She'd been through the first-floor rooms only twice before. First on her initial viewing to take notes and measurements. The second time to recheck them. But there were no workmen now, no sounds of voices or hammering.

She slipped into the room beyond the parlor, dreaming a bit.

This would be the library—glossy shelves filled with books, deep-cushioned chairs inviting a guest to curl up to read. A library table would stand there, she mused, a Sheraton if she could find one, with a decanter of brandy, a vase of seasonal flowers, an old pewter inkwell.

Library steps, of course, she continued visualizing, seeing it all perfectly, almost to the grain of wood. And the wide-backed chairs near the crackling fire would need cozy footstools.

She wanted a reading stand in the far corner, one with a cabriole base. She'd set a big, old Bible with gilt-edged pages open on it.

Abigail O'Brian, married to Charles Richard Barlow, April 10, 1856
Catherine Anne Barlow, born June 5, 1857
Charles Richard Barlow, Junior, born November 22, 1859
Robert Michael Barlow, born February 9, 1861
Abigail Barlow, died September 18, 1864

Regan shivered, swayed. She came back to herself slowly, her arms wrapped tight to ward off the sudden, bitter cold, her heart pounding as the vision faded from in front of her eyes.

How had she known that? she wondered, running a shaky hand over her face. Where had those names and dates come from?

She'd read them somewhere, she assured herself, but shuddered again. All the research she'd done, of course she'd read them. Very slowly, she backed out of the room and stood in the hall to catch her breath.

Of course she'd known the Barlows of that time had had three children. She'd looked it up. The dates must have been there, as well—she'd retained them for some reason, that was all.

Not for anything would she have admitted that she had thought, just for a moment, that she'd actually seen the thick white page of a Bible opened, and the names and dates written there in a carefully formal hand.

She walked to the stairs and climbed them.

He'd left the door open this time. When she reached the landing, she heard the scrape of his trowel against the wall. Letting out a relieved breath, she crossed the hall.

And was warm again, just looking at him.

"Need a hand?"

He glanced back, saw her standing there in her classic sweater and pleated trousers. "Not in that outfit. I just wanted to get this coat finished, and I thought you needed some sleep."

She contented herself with leaning against the doorway to watch him. "Why is it that manual labor is so attractive on some men?"

"Some women like to see guys sweat."

"Apparently I do." Thoughtfully she studied his technique, the slide of the trowel, the flick of the wrist. "You know, you're better at this than the guy who did my place over the shop. Very tidy."

"I hate drywall work."

"Then why are you doing it?"

"I like when it's finished. And I'm faster than the team I hired."

"How did you learn?"

"We were always having to fix something out at the farm." He twisted his neck, cracking out kinks. "When I left, I did a lot of handyman stuff."

"Then started your own company."

"I don't like working for somebody else."

"Neither do I." She hesitated, waiting while he

scraped off his tools. "Where did you go? When you left?"

"South." He stooped to bang the top back on the bucket of compound. "Picked up some jobs here and there. Figured out I was better at swinging a hammer than running a plow." Out of habit, he reached into his shirt pocket, found it empty. Swore. "Quit smoking," he muttered.

"Good for you."

"It's driving me nuts." To keep himself busy, he walked over to check a seam he'd finished the night before.

"You went to Florida," she said prompting him.

"Yeah, that's where I ended up. Lots of construction work in Florida. I started buying houses—dumps—fixing them up, turning them over. Did pretty well. So I came back." He turned to her. "That's about it."

"I wasn't prying," she began.

"I didn't say you were. There just isn't much to it, Regan. I had a rep when I left here. Spent my last night in town in a bar fight. With Joe Dolin."

"I wondered if there was history there," she murmured.

"Not much of one." He slipped off the bandanna

he'd twisted at his forehead to keep the hair out of his eyes, stuffed it in his pocket. "We just hated each other's guts."

"I'd say your taste in enemies is excellent."

Restless again, he moved his shoulders. "If it hadn't been him, it would have been somebody else. I was in the mood that night." His grin flashed, but there wasn't much humor in it. "Hell, I was usually in the mood to cause trouble. Nobody ever figured I'd amount to anything, not even me."

If he was trying to tell her something, she wasn't sure she quite understood it. "It looks as though they were wrong. Even you."

"People are going to talk, about us." He'd thought about it, as he watched her sleep, finding himself restless and edgy and needing to move. "You're going to walk into Ed's or Kingston's Market, and conversation's going to take a hitch. And when you walk out again, people are going to start talking about what that nice Bishop woman is doing with that troublemaker Rafe MacKade."

"I've been here three years, Rafe. I know how it works."

He needed something to do with his hands, so he

picked up sandpaper and attacked the first dry seam. "I don't imagine you've given them much to gossip about up to now."

He worked as if the devil were looking over his shoulder, she thought. It seemed he did everything with that controlled urgency just under the surface.

"I was pretty hot news when I opened the shop. What's this flatlander doing taking over old Leroy's place, selling antiques instead of screws and pipe fittings?" She smiled a little. "That got me a lot of browsers, and a good many browsers became customers." She angled her head, watching him. "Something like this should pick business up dramatically for a few weeks."

"I want you to understand what you're getting into."

"It's a little late for that." Because she sensed he needed some prodding, she obliged. "Maybe you're worried about your reputation."

"Right." Dust flew as he sanded. "I was thinking of running for mayor."

"No, your bad-boy rep. 'MacKade must be getting soft, hanging around that nice Bishop woman. Next thing you know, he'll be buying flowers instead of a six-pack. Bet she'll whip him into shape.'"

Curious, he tossed the sandpaper aside, tucked his thumbs in his front pockets and turned to look at her. "Is that what you're going to try to do, Regan? Whip me into shape?"

"Is that what you're worried about, MacKade? That I could?"

It wasn't a comfortable thought. "Legions have tried." He walked over, skimmed a dusty finger down her cheek. "It'd be easier for me to corrupt you, darling. I could have you playing nine-ball at Duff's Tavern in no time."

"I could have you quoting Shelley."

"Shelley who?"

With a chuckle, she rose on her toes to give him a friendly kiss. "Percy Bysshe Shelley. Better watch yourself."

The idea of that was so ridiculous, his tensed shoulders relaxed. "Darling, the day I start spouting poetry's the day Shane's prize hog sprouts wings and flies down Main Street."

She smiled again, kissed him again. "You don't want to make it a bet. Come on, I'd like to take a look at the work in progress."

He snatched her hand. "What kind of bet?"

She laughed, tugged him into the hall. "Rafe, I'm joking. Give me a tour."

"Just hold on. MacKades never back down from a dare."

"I'm daring you to quote Shelley?" She sighed, shook her head. "Okay, I dare you."

"No, that's not how it works." Considering, he lifted her hand, nibbled on her fingers. The flicker of arousal in her eyes inspired him. "I say I can have you so crazy about me within a month that you'll wiggle into a leather miniskirt. A red one. Walk into the tavern for beer and nine-ball."

Arousal turned quickly into amusement. "What odd fantasies you have, MacKade. Can you actually see me in some tarty little skirt, playing pool?"

The smile turned wicked. "Oh, yeah. I can see that just fine. Make sure you wear those really high heels, too. The skinny ones."

"I never wear leather without stilettos. Anything less would be tacky."

"And no bra."

Her laughed puffed out. "Really into this, aren't you?"

"I'm getting there. You'll do it, too." He cupped a

hand on her hip to nudge her closer. "Because you'll be crazy about me."

"It's obvious one of us has already lost his mind. Okay." Not one to refuse a challenge, she put a hand on his chest, pushed him back. "I say within that same period of time, I'll have you on your knees, clutching a bouquet of…ah…lilacs—"

"Lilacs?"

"Yes, I'm very fond of lilacs. You'll quote Shelley like a champ."

"What's the winner get?"

"Satisfaction."

He had to smile. "That ought to be enough. Deal."

They shook hands on it. "Am I going to get that tour now?"

"Sure." He draped an arm around her shoulders and entertained himself with the vision of those very fine legs beneath a tight red skirt. "We went with your idea of a kind of bridal suite." He led the way down the hall, opened a six-paneled door. "Just about ready for trim work in here."

"Rafe." Delighted, she stepped inside.

The delicate floral wallpaper was nearly all hung. The coffered ceiling gleamed with fresh paint. French doors were in place, and would one day open onto the wide porch, overlook gardens in riotous bloom. The floor was covered with drop cloths, but she could imagine it glossy and accented with a lovely faded tapestry rug.

She stepped around buckets and ladders, already arranging furniture in her head. "It's going to be beautiful," she murmured.

"It's coming along." He lifted a tarp from the fireplace. "The mantel was shot. I couldn't fix it. Found a good piece of yellow pine, though. The woodworker's using the original as a guide."

"That rose-colored trim is going to be wonderful in here." She looked through an adjoining doorway. "And this is the bath."

"Mmm…" He studied the room over her shoulder. It was good-sized, and the plumbers had roughed it in. "Used to be a dressing room."

She reached for his hand, gripped it. "Can you smell it?"

"Roses." Absently he rubbed his cheek over her hair. "It always smells like roses in here. One of the paper hangers accused his partner of wearing perfume."

"This was her room, wasn't it? Abigail's. She died in here."

"Probably. Hey." He tipped up her face, watched uncomfortably as a tear trailed down her cheek. "Don't."

"It's so sad. She must have been terribly unhappy. Knowing the man she'd married, the father of her children, was capable of such cold-blooded cruelty. How did he treat her, Rafe? Did he love her, or did he only own her?"

"There's no way to know. Don't cry." Awkward, he brushed the tear away. "It makes me feel like I have six thumbs. I mean it." For lack of something better to do, he patted her head. "There's no use crying over something that happened more than a hundred years ago."

"But she's still here." Wrapping her arms around him, Regan snuggled into his chest. "I feel so sorry for her, for all of them."

"You're not going to do yourself, or me, any good if you get tangled up every time you come in here."

"I know." She sighed, comforted by the way his heart beat strong and steady against her. "It's odd how you get used to it, a little bit at a time. Rafe, when I was downstairs alone..."

"What?" Uneasy, he tilted her face toward his again. "It's nothing."

"What?" he repeated, giving her chin a little shake.

"Well, I walked into the library. What was the library," she went on, torn between the need to tell him and embarrassment. "What will be the library. And I— Rafe, I could see it."

His eyes were sharp, narrowed, totally concentrated. "See what?"

"The room. Not the stained floors and the new wiring you've put in. The room. Books on the wall, flowers on the table, drapes at the windows. I could really see it," she repeated, her own brow creasing. "Not the way I do in my head when I'm planning things out. Not exactly like that. I was thinking to myself, sort of projecting, I suppose. I imagined this, well, I thought I was imagining a Bible stand, with an old family Bible opened on it. And I could read the page, almost touch it. Marriage and births and death."

She took time to catch her breath. "You're not saying anything."

"Because I'm listening to you."

"I know it sounds crazy."

"Not in this house, it doesn't."

"It was so reàl, so sad. The way the scent of roses in this room is real, and sad. Then it was so cold, bitter, like a window had been flung open to the weather."

She moved her shoulders, laid her head on his chest again. "That's all."

"That's a lot for one day." Wanting to soothe, he stroked his hand over her hair. "I can give Devin a call, have him come get you."

"No, I don't want to leave. It shook me for a moment, but it's just as I said before. You get to accept it. I can handle it."

"I shouldn't have left you alone."

"Don't be silly. I don't need to be guarded against grieving ghosts."

But he wanted to guard her. He wished she had called for him. It surprised him just how much he wished she had needed him enough to call out for him.

"Next time you want to go in the library, let me know. I'll go with you."

"The house is already changing," she said quietly. "You've done that by caring for it. I like feeling I've had a part in that, too."

"You have." He pressed his lips to her hair.

"When people live in it, make love in it, laugh in it, it'll change again. The house needs people."

She shifted, lifted her mouth to his. "Make love with me."

He cupped her face in his hands, deepened the kiss. When he picked her up, carried her from the room, the scent of roses followed. She looped her arms around him, pressed her lips to his throat. Already her blood was heating, already her pulse was pounding.

"It's like a drug," she murmured.

"I know." He stopped at the top of the stairs, found her mouth again.

"I've never been like this before." Swamped with emotions, she turned her face into his shoulder.

Neither had he, he thought.

As he carried her down, neither noticed that the air had remained warm and calm.

He laid her in front of the fire. Levering himself up on his elbow, he traced the shape of her face with a fingertip. Something kindled inside her, simmered with desire and flamed around her heart.

"Rafe."

"Ssh…"

To quiet her, he brushed his lips over her brow. She

didn't know what she would have said, was grateful he'd stopped her. The wanting was more than enough. She could be relieved that neither of them needed words.

She should have been relieved.

Her mouth was ready for his, and it warmed beautifully under the pressure of lips and tongue. Though desire remained, poised and trembling, everything in her seemed to soften.

Here was tenderness, so sweet, so unexpected. Her sigh whispered out like a secret.

He felt the change, in her, in himself. Marveled at it. Why had they always been in such a hurry? he wondered. Why had he hesitated to savor, and be savored, when there was so much here?

He loved the flavor of her, that quietly seductive taste that clung to her skin. The feel of her, soft curves, long lines. The smell of her hair, her clothes, her shoulders.

So he savored it now, all of it, with long, slow kisses that clouded his mind and made him forget there was anything beyond this room for either of them.

His hands were careful this time as he drew her sweater off, slipped the trousers down her hips. Rather than touch, rather than take, he kissed her again, drawing out the simple meeting of lips until her body went limp.

"Let me." With a dreamy murmur, she shifted until they were both kneeling. Already clouded, her eyes stayed on his while she unbuttoned his shirt. Trapped in the silky mood, she slipped it away and, with her hands resting lightly on his shoulders, swayed to him.

They held each other, moving only for quiet, sipping tastes, soft, gentle caresses. She smiled when his lips brushed her shoulder, sighed when hers tasted his throat.

When they were naked, he drew her down so that she lay over him, so that her hair fell to curtain them both.

She could have floated on this whisper-thin cloud of sensations endlessly, with the winter sun slanting cold light through the windows, the fire crackling, his body strong and hard beneath hers.

The feel of his hands on her, stroking, soothing even as they aroused, was like a gift. She felt the wonder of it in every pore, in every nerve, with every pulse.

There was no clash and fury now, no desperation, no vicious drive to mate. Now she was aware of everything—the dust motes spinning in the sunbeam that rayed over the floor, the sedate hiss of flame on wood, the scent of roses and man.

She could count his heartbeats, quicker, stronger, as her lips trailed over his chest. The bunching and quivering of a muscle beneath her hand, the sound of her own thickening breath.

With a sigh that caught in her throat, she wrapped around him as he rolled her to her back.

Time spun out, stretched, quivered. The clock on the mantel ticked the seconds away, and the minutes. But that was another world. Here there were only needs lazily satisfied, and hearts quietly lost.

For pleasure—his as well as hers—he eased her gently to the edge and over. His name was only a murmur on her lips as she arched, tensed, softened to silk. She opened for him, drawing him close with a velvety moan as he slipped into her.

Overwhelmed by her, by the simplicity of it, he burrowed his face in her hair. The tenderness shattered them both.

They didn't speak of it. When they parted in the morning, both of them were determinedly casual. But they thought of it. And they worried.

Rafe watched her drive off as the sun struggled over the mountains to the east. When she was gone, when there was no one to see, he rubbed the heel of his hand over his heart.

There was an ache there that he couldn't quite will away. He had a very bad feeling that she was the cause of it, and that somehow, in a matter of hours, he'd gotten in over his head.

God, he missed her already.

He swore at himself for that, then swore again for reaching like a trained dog for the cigarettes that weren't there. Both were just habits, he assured himself. If he wanted, he could just go buy a pack of cigarettes and smoke his brains out. Just as he could snatch her back anytime.

Sex was a powerful bond. It wasn't surprising it had caught him, as well.

It didn't have to be any more than that. They'd tidied that up, hadn't they? A man was entitled to be a little shaky after thirty-odd hours of sex and solitude with a gorgeous woman.

He didn't want anything more. Neither did she.

It was a relief and a pleasure to find a lover who wanted no more and no less than he did himself. A woman who didn't expect him to play games, make promises neither expected to be kept, say words that were only words, after all.

Scowling, he grabbed a shovel and began to deal with the snow that piled the walk. The sun was strengthening, and he worked fast, so that even with the bite of the northern wind he sweated satisfactorily under his coat.

She'd probably head straight for the shower, he mused, tossing heavy snow off the path. Wash that pretty doe-colored hair of hers.

He wondered what it looked like wet.

She'd dig some of those neat, classy clothes out of her closet. Nope, he thought, correcting himself. Regan would never dig. She'd select. Quiet colors, simple lines. One of those professional-woman's jackets, with a pin on the lapel.

She'd fix her face, nothing too obvious. Just hints of blush along the cheekbones, a touch of color above those ridiculously long lashes. Then lipstick—not red, not pink, a kind of rose that accented those full lips and that sassy little mole beside them.

Halfway down the walk, he stopped, leaned against

the shovel and wondered if he was losing his mind. He was actually thinking about her makeup.

What the hell did he care what paint she slapped on before she went down to open the shop?

She'd put on the kettle for tea, or have cider simmering so that the place smelled of apples and spices. Then she'd go through the day without giving him a thought.

Snow flew as he attacked it. Well, he had plenty to do himself, and no time to brood about her.

He'd reached the end of the walk, and the end of his patience, when Devin rattled up the lane in the sheriff's cruiser.

"What the hell do you want?" Rafe shouted. "Haven't you got somebody to arrest?"

"Funny how a little blizzard quiets things down." Leaning on the open car door, Devin watched his brother with amusement. "Saw Regan's car was gone, figured it was safe to drop by."

"I've got men due any minute. I don't have time to chat."

"In that case, I'll take my doughnuts and go."

Rafe swiped a hand over his chilled face. "What kind?"

"Apple and brown sugar."

Some things were sacred, and an apple doughnut on a cold morning topped the list.

"Well, are you going to stand there all morning with that idiot grin on your face? Give me a damn doughnut."

Obligingly, Devin took the bag out of the car and sauntered over. "Had three fender benders in town yesterday from people not smart enough to stay put."

"Antietam's a wild town, all right. Have to shoot anybody?"

"Not lately." Devin took out a doughnut for himself before passing the bag to Rafe. "Broke up a fist-fight, though."

"Down at the tavern?"

"Nope, at the market. Millie Yeader and Mrs. Metz were going at it over the last pack of toilet paper."

Rafe's lips twitched. "People get a little nervous over necessities when a big snow hits."

"Tell me about it. Miz Metz conked Millie with a bunch of bananas. Took a lot of diplomacy to keep Millie from filing charges."

"Assault with tropical fruit. Could've done hard time for that." Calm again, Rafe licked apple from his thumb. "Did you come by to give me the latest trials and tribulations of Antietam?"

"That's just a bonus." Devin polished off his doughnut, reached for a cigarette. His grin was wide and unsympathetic when Rafe groaned. He lit it, inhaled lavishly. "I hear food tastes better when you quit."

"Nothing's better," Rafe shot back. "But some of us have real willpower. Blow it over here, you bastard."

"Secondhand smoke's the real killer," Devin told him, and blew a stream in Rafe's direction. "You look a little out of sorts, Rafe. Trouble in paradise?"

Rafe gave some thought to beating his brother to death with the snow shovel and stealing all his cigarettes. Reminding himself it was all a matter of self-control, he leaned on the shovel, instead.

"How long did it take Shane to open his big mouth?"

"Let's see." Considering, Devin smoked and studied the landscape. "The way the roads were yesterday, I'd say it took him, oh, about seven minutes to get from here to my office." He flicked ash aside. "Let's say seven minutes and ten seconds."

"Now you're here to offer your sage advice?"

"Hey, it was pretty sage to talk those two snarling women into splitting the six-pack of pink toilet paper. But no." With a self-deprecating smile, he took a last drag, then flicked the cigarette away.

Rafe watched it wistfully as it hissed in the snow.

"I'm not exactly the expert on romance in the MacKade family." Devin's grin was crooked, and didn't last long. "I thought you might like the latest on Joe Dolin."

"He's locked up."

"For now. I got word he's copping to second-degree assault. If he listens to his lawyer, he'll agree to alcohol counseling. He'll get a fine, suspended sentence with probation, and a stern warning not to hit his wife again."

"What the hell kind of deal is that?"

"Prisons are crowded. Domestic disputes don't usually equal tough sentencing. He says 'Yeah, I did it, I'm sorry. I lost my temper, I was drunk, I lost my job. My self-esteem is really low.' The judge says 'Get yourself into counseling, my boy, and sin no more.'"

Rafe studied his brother's face. Beneath the calm,

he caught the twitches of fury and frustration. "You're just going to let it go at that?"

"I don't sentence." Devin struggled to bite back on his sense of anger and impotence. "There's nothing I can do except talk Cassie into letting me issue a restraining order, and make sure he doesn't get near her or the kids."

"Meanwhile, they're bunked down at Regan's. That puts her in the middle."

"I don't like it any better than you do. I've got the law to work around."

"I don't."

Devin's gaze was cool and level. "No, you don't. But you start something with Dolin, and it's going to come down in his favor. He'll make a mistake, Rafe. All it takes is one, and I'll have him caged again. Until I do… I don't know where things stand between you and Regan, but if you were staying there, it'd hold a lot more weight with me than some useless restraining order."

"You want me to ask Regan to let me move in with her?"

"And Cassie, and the kids."

The idea was surprisingly appealing. Waking up beside her, sharing that first cup of coffee. "You going to deputize me, Dev?"

"Not on your life."

"Too bad. Well, I'll run it by Regan and let you know."

Chapter 8

"Absolutely not." Regan planted her feet, folded her arms over her chest. "You are not sleeping in my bed with two little children in the next room."

"This isn't about sex," Rafe said patiently. "That's just a bonus. I'm telling you, this is an official request from the sheriff."

"Who just happens to be your brother. No." She turned away to set glassware back on the shelf she'd been dusting. "It would make Cassie uncomfortable and set a poor example for the children."

And if they weren't there? He found the question leaping to the tip of his tongue like a frog. He was barely in time to prevent himself from letting it jump out.

"It's Cassie and the kids who are the issue," he insisted. "You think Dolin's just going to leave them alone because Cassie signs some paper telling him to?"

"I have no idea what he'll do, but he'll have to get past me first."

The thought of it, just the thought of it, had his blood icing over. "Now you listen…"

She jerked his hand from her shoulder and whirled back. "No, *you* listen. The man is a bully and a drunk. I'm not afraid of drunken bullies. I offered Cassie my home, and she's welcome to stay there as long as she wants. I have a good solid lock on the door, which I'll use. I know the number for the sheriff's office, which I'll use, as well, if it's necessary."

"There's no lock on that door." Rafe jerked a thumb toward the front of the shop. "What's to stop him from walking in here during business hours and harassing you? Or worse."

"I am."

"Right." He wondered if shaking her would rattle her brains back into place. "Putting Dolin on the receiving end of that stubborn chin of yours isn't going to stop him. In case you haven't figured it out, he likes hurting women."

"I'll take a moment to remind you that for the past three years I've been here and you haven't. I've seen exactly what he's done to Cassie."

"And you figure because you're not married to him, you're safe?" He did shake her. "You can't be that stupid."

"I'm not stupid," she shot back. "I'm competent. I don't need or want you for a bodyguard."

His eyes changed, going from full heat to slow burn. On her shoulders, his hands tensed, then lifted away.

"I guess that's the bottom line, isn't it? You don't need or want my help."

Ego, she thought with a muffled sigh. There was no monster so fierce or so vulnerable as a man's ego. "The sheriff's office is five minutes away, if I need to call out troops." Hoping to calm them both, Regan put her hands on his shoulders. "Rafe, I appreciate your concern, really I do. But I can take care of myself, and Cassie, too, if it comes to that."

"I bet you can."

"I worked a shop in D.C. for years. One memorable evening, I was robbed at gunpoint. I know how to be sensible, how not to take chances and how to defend myself. I appreciate the fact that you're worried, but I'm not Cassie. He can't frighten or intimidate me."

"Regan—"

"Wait, let me finish. Cassie is so fragile right now, and the children are too quiet. I'm not sure how they would handle having a man around. The kids don't know you."

He jammed his hands in his pockets. "I'm not going to kick them around."

"They don't know that. Little Emma sits at Cassie's feet with her doll and barely says a word. And the boy— God, Rafe, he breaks my heart. They need time to feel safe again. You're too big, you're too strong, you're too…male."

Stubbornly he ignored the fact that she'd hurt him— that he could be hurt—and concentrated on the situation at hand. "You're being pigheaded."

"I'm doing what seems right to me. That's the only way I know how to handle things. Believe me, I've thought this through, weighed the options. Having you move in just isn't one of them."

"Invite me to dinner," he said abruptly.

"You want to come to dinner?"

"Ask me to dinner, so I can get to know the kids, so they'll get used to me being around."

"Now who's pigheaded?" But she sighed. It was a reasonable compromise. "All right, seven-thirty, and you're out by ten."

"Can we neck on the couch after the kids go to bed?"

"Maybe. Now go away."

"Aren't you going to kiss me goodbye?"

She huffed out a breath, then kissed him primly on the cheek. "Business hours," she said, then laughed when he grabbed her. "Rafe, we're right in front of the window. I—"

The rest was lost as he crushed his mouth to hers. "Might as well give them something to talk about." And give her something to think about, he told himself. She was damn well going to do a lot of thinking about Rafe MacKade.

He nipped her lip, let her go, then sauntered out the door.

A block away, Cassie sat in Devin's office, twisting her hands together. She knew it should be easier because it was Devin, someone she'd known all her life. But it only made the shame worse.

"I'm sorry, we got busy, and I couldn't take my break until now."

"That's all right, Cassie." It had become habit to keep his voice quiet when he spoke to her, as a man might speak to a wounded bird. "I've got the paperwork filled out for you. You just have to sign it."

"He's not going to go to jail."

A fist squeezed his heart at the emptiness in her tone. "No."

"Is it because I let him hit me?"

"No." He wished he could reach out to soothe those nervous hands. But the desk was between them, an official barrier. "He admitted that he hurt you, but the court took other things into consideration. His drinking problem, his loss of a longtime job. He'll have to go into counseling, report to his probation officer. Stay out of trouble."

"It could be good for him." She looked up, then, just as quickly, down again. "The counseling. If he stops drinking, maybe everything would be all right."

"Yeah." And he could run a Popsicle stand in hell,

Devin thought. "In the meantime, you need to protect yourself. That's what the restraining order's for."

She lifted her gaze again, and this time her eyes held his. "That paper is going to keep him from coming back?"

Devin grabbed a cigarette out of his pack, then tossed it down. When he spoke, his voice was cool and official. "This bars him from coming near you. He can't come into the diner when you're working there. He can't approach you on the street, or come to Regan's house as long as you're staying there. If he breaks any one of the regulations set down here, he'll void his parole and serve the eighteen months."

"He knows about this?"

"He's been notified."

She moistened her lips. He couldn't come near her. The idea whirled around in her head. If he couldn't come near her, he couldn't hit her.

"I only have to sign it."

"Yes, you only have to sign it." Devin rose then, came around the desk to offer her a pen. When she made no move to take it, he bit back an oath. "Cassie, what do you want? Can you just tell me what you want?"

She shook her head, took the pen. She signed her

name quickly, as though it hurt. "I know I've put you through a lot of trouble, Devin."

"It's my job," he said shortly.

"You're a good sheriff." When he glanced back, obviously surprised, she tried to smile. "You are, quiet and competent and good with people. Everyone knows they can count on you. My mother always said you and your brothers would end up behind bars." She flushed and stared down at the floor. "I'm sorry. That was stupid."

"No, it wasn't. I used to think the same myself." He smiled then, because just for a moment she'd sounded like the girl he remembered. "You know, Cass, that's about the longest little speech I've heard out of you in close to ten years."

"I'm always putting my foot in my mouth."

"Don't do that." He'd taken her chin to lift her head before he realized he meant to—before she flinched like a startled doe. Moving with care, he dropped his hand, eased a hip on the corner of the desk. "How are the kids?"

"They're all right. Better."

"Getting along all right at Regan's?"

"She's wonderful. I forget I'm imposing, because

she makes everything so normal. She and Rafe—"
She broke off, her color rising again. "You've got better things to do than listen to me gossip."

"No, I don't." He'd have done anything to keep her talking. To keep her there. "What do you think about them? Regan and Rafe?"

"I— She looked happy when she came home this morning."

"He looked miserable when I dropped by the house this morning."

Her smile was slow and shy. "That's a good sign. Rafe always needed a woman who could make him unhappy. It was always too easy for him. For all of you."

"Was it?" Thoughtful, he picked up his cigarette again, ran it through his fingers. "I remember you turned me down."

"Oh." Fumbling, she rose. "That was a hundred years ago."

"Not quite twelve. You were sweet sixteen."

"I was going with Joe." As she tugged on her coat, she wondered if she'd really ever been sixteen. "I can't even remember who we were then, or what we were looking for. Thanks, Devin, for taking care of this."

"That's what I'm here for, to take care of things."

At the door, she paused, but didn't look back. It was easier to speak if she didn't have to look into those cool, pitying eyes. "You asked me what I wanted, Devin. I just want to feel safe." She said it so quietly, he barely heard. "That's really all."

In a coat that was too thin to fight off the biting wind, she walked back to the café.

Rafe arrived ten minutes early for dinner and squirmed on Regan's doorstep like a nervous suitor. He had a bottle of wine in one hand and a bakery box of cookies designed to win the kids over in the other.

He wished he'd remembered before his brainstorm that he knew nothing about people under the age of sixteen.

As a test, he turned the knob. It was somewhat satisfying to find it locked tight. He knocked sharply, stepped back. It was Regan who opened it, as far as the thick security chain allowed.

"Okay, so far you're passing. But you should have asked who it was first."

"I looked out the window." She shut the door in his face, then, after a rattle of chain, opened it. "I had the feeling there'd be a quiz." Smiling, she studied the offerings. "No lilacs?"

"No chance." He would have kissed her if he hadn't noticed the solemn gray eyes watching him from the cushions of the sofa. "Looks like you've got a mouse in the house."

Regan jerked, then smiled when she saw Emma. "She's quiet as one, but prettier. Emma, this is Mr. MacKade. You met him at Ed's, remember?" Regan held out a hand. Eyeing him warily, Emma slipped from the couch.

She was five, Rafe knew, and tiny as a fairy princess, with her mother's pale hair and smoky eyes.

"I knew your mama when she was your age," he told her.

Emma darted behind Regan's legs and peered up at him.

Knowing it was a shameless bribe, he shook the bakery box. "Want a cookie, honey?"

That earned him the faintest of smiles, but Regan took the box out of his hands. "Not before dinner."

"Spoilsport. But dinner smells good."

"Cassie's chicken and dumplings. I had to practically tie her down to keep her from taking the kids and eating at the diner. We compromised and had her cook dinner. Come on, Emma, we'll take the cookies in the kitchen."

With one hand clutching Regan's slacks, Emma darted looks over her shoulder.

She thought he was big, but his eyes weren't mean. She'd already learned how to read eyes. And he looked a lot like the sheriff, who sometimes picked her up and gave her lemon drops.

But Emma watched her mother carefully to gauge her reaction to the man.

Cassie looked up from the stove and smiled. "Hi, Rafe."

He moved to her, lightly kissed her bruised cheek. "How's it going?"

"Fine, everything's fine." She laid a hand on the shoulder of the boy beside her. "Connor, you remember Mr. MacKade."

"Nice to see you again, Connor." Rafe offered a hand. The little boy with the pale hair and the dusky blue eyes shook hands hesitantly. "You'd be, what, in third, fourth grade?"

"Third, yes, sir."

Rafe lifted a brow and passed the bottle of wine to

Regan. That would make him about eight, Rafe figured, and the kid spoke as quietly as an old priest. "Miz Witt still teaching there?"

"Yes, sir."

"We used to call her Miz Dimwit." When the boy's eyes widened, Rafe plucked a carrot from beside the salad bowl. "Bet you still do."

"Yes, sir," Connor mumbled, slanting a look at his mother. "Sometimes." Screwing up the courage he'd worked on building ever since he'd been told Rafe MacKade was coming, Connor drew in his breath. "You bought the Barlow Place."

"That's right."

"It's haunted."

Rafe bit off some carrot and grinned. "You bet."

"I know all about the battle and everything," Connor said in one quick burst. "It was the bloodiest day of the Civil War, and nobody really won, because—" He broke off, embarrassed. This, he thought miserably, was why some of the kids called him nerdhead in school.

"Because nobody went for the final push," Rafe finished for him. "Maybe you'd like to come by the house sometime, take a look. I could use somebody who knows all about the battle."

"I've got a book. With pictures."

"Yeah?" Rafe took the wine Regan offered him. "Let's see."

It was simple enough to draw the boy out, as long as they were discussing McClellan's flawed strategy or the Battle of Burnside Bridge. Rafe saw a bright, needy boy, too bookish to fit neatly with his contemporaries, too shy to showcase his own brain.

The girl, a miniature of her mother, never strayed far from Cassie or Regan, ate her dinner in small, neat bites. And watched him like a baby hawk.

"Ed would be better off having you in the kitchen than waiting tables," Rafe commented after he'd polished off a second helping. "Her business would double in a month."

Off guard, Cassie blinked at him. No one had complimented her cooking in too many years to count. "I'm glad you liked it. I could put some of the leftovers in a dish for you. You'd just have to heat them up."

"I'll take them."

When Cassie rose and began to clear, Regan held up a hand. "No, you don't. You cooked, I clear."

"But—"

"That was the deal. And since Rafe ate enough for two growing boys, he can help."

The Dolins looked on, awed, as Rafe cheerfully stacked plates. The men they knew would have belched, loosened their belts and plopped down in front of the TV with a six-pack.

"Daddy says girls and sissies do dishes," Emma announced, in a surprisingly clear voice.

"Emma!" Paling, Cassie stared at Rafe and waited for the retribution.

He considered making a comment about her father's brains but decided against it. "My mama always said a meal has to be earned." He said it lightly and winked at her. "And if I do the dishes with Regan, I'll probably be able to kiss her."

"Why?"

"Because she tastes almost as good as your mama's chicken and dumplings."

Satisfied with that, Emma nibbled solemnly on her cookie.

"I'll just give Emma her bath, then." Flustered, Cassie shooed her children along. "I have to turn in early. I have the breakfast shift in the morning."

"Thanks for dinner, Cassie."

"You handled that very well," Regan murmured. "That's probably the first time in years they've sat at the dinner table with a man and had a civilized conversation."

"Dolin's not only a swine, he's a fool." Rafe set stacked plates on the kitchen counter. "Sweet woman like that, beautiful kids. Any man would be lucky to have them."

A home of your own, Rafe mused. A woman who loved you. Kids racing out to meet you at the end of the day. Family meals around a table. Noise in the kitchen.

Funny, he'd never thought that was something he'd wanted, or needed.

"You made an impression," Regan went on as she filled the sink with hot, soapy water. "A good one. I can't think of anything better for all of them than seeing a strong, intelligent man behaving in a strong, intelligent way."

She glanced back, and her smile faltered at the look in his eye. She was used to the way he stared at her, or she nearly was. But this was different, deeper.

"What is it?"

"Hmm?" He caught himself, realized he felt like

a man who had nearly skidded hard and landed on very thin ice. "Nothing. It's nothing." Good God, he'd actually been thinking about marriage and kids and picket fences. "The boy, Connor. He's awfully bright, isn't he?"

"Straight *A*s," Regan said, as proudly as if he were her own. "He's bright, sensitive and sweet—which made him a perfect target for Joe. The man bullied the poor kid mercilessly."

"He hit him?" The question was mild, but the fire was already burning.

"No, I don't think so. Cassie's fiercely protective of her children. But emotional abuse doesn't leave bruises." She shrugged. "Well, they're out of it now." She handed him a plate to dry. "Did your father do dishes?"

"Only on Thanksgiving." Rafe polished off the plate, set it aside. "Buck MacKade was a man's man."

"Buck?" Impressed, Regan pursed her lips. "Sounds formidable."

"He was tough. Had eyes that could drill holes in you if you messed up. Devin got his eyes. I got his hands." Bemused, Rafe stared down at his palms, flexed his fingers. "It was a hell of a surprise to me when I looked down one day and saw my father's hands on the end of my arms."

She couldn't have said why it touched her so to see him smiling down at his hands, a dishcloth tossed over his shoulder. "You were close to him?"

"Not close enough. Not for long enough."

"When did you lose him?"

"I was fifteen. Tractor rolled on him. It took him a week to die."

She plunged her hands into the water again, struggled with tears. "Is that why you hate the farm?"

"Yeah, I guess it is." Odd, he'd never realized it was that simple, that direct. The farm had taken his father, so he had to hate the farm. "He loved it, every rocky acre. The way Shane does."

"What did Jared get from him?"

"The mouth—Jared can horse-trade just like the old man, and make you think you got the best end of the deal."

"Then I'm relieved he's my lawyer." She offered another plate. "My father never did a dish in his life. I'm sure my mother would be horrified if he tried. The kitchen is a woman's domain," she said dryly. "They agree on that completely. She brings him his first cup of coffee every morning before he goes to the hospital. He's a surgeon."

"Hard feelings?"

"I used to have them," she admitted. "She made herself into exactly the woman he wanted her to be. If she was ever anything else, wanted to be anything else, anything more, it doesn't show. She's Dr. Bishop's wife, and that's all."

He began to see just why she was so set on marking her own boundaries, taking her own stands. "Maybe that's all she wants to be."

"Apparently. It just infuriated me to see the way she catered to him, the way he patted her on the head. He actually gives her an allowance and calls her 'the little woman.'"

It still made her grit her teeth. "She loved living in D.C., but a few years ago when he decided that he wanted to relocate to Arizona, she packed up without a murmur." Regan sighed. "But they're blissfully happy. I baffle them as much as they baffle me."

"Because you don't have a rich husband, a big house and a membership at the country club."

"Exactly." Surprised and amused, she glanced at him. "Have you met them?"

"I think I just did." And, in doing so, caught a fresh new glimpse of her. "So, darling, why don't you have a rich husband, a big house and a membership at the country club?"

"Because I like independence, my own space and my golf game is dreadful." She shook back her hair. "Actually, my mother had high hopes for me when she met Jared."

The bowl he was drying clattered when he set it down. "Run through that again."

"They came to visit right after the settlement. He took us out to dinner."

"Jared," Rafe said carefully, "took you out to dinner."

"Mmm-hmm… A couple of times. My mother really liked the idea that I was seeing a lawyer. Next-best thing to a doctor, in her mind."

"Seeing. As in dating. You dated Jared?"

"We went out a few times. It was right after his divorce." She held out another bowl, lifting a brow when he made no move to take it. "Is there a problem?"

"You dated my brother?"

"I believe we just established that." She decided it

was a better idea to bite the inside of her lip than to let it curve. "Didn't he mention it?"

"No. I think I'd like your definition of *date*."

"You mean, did I sleep with him?" Struggling to keep her face composed, she tilted her head. "Are you going to go beat him up, big guy? Can I come watch?"

Obviously she didn't know how close she was to having her pretty face dumped in dishwater. "It's a simple question."

"You've got a muscle twitching in your jaw, Rafe. It looks good on you. No," she said, and then she did laugh. "Of course I didn't sleep with him." Enjoying herself, she shoved the bowl into his hands. "I did kiss him good-night. A couple of times. I'm now in the position to state, unequivocally, that at least fifty percent of the MacKade brothers are champion kissers."

"Think twice before you try for a hundred percent—or even seventy-five." He set the bowl aside, picked up his wine. "Why didn't you sleep with him?"

"Really, Rafe." She rolled her eyes. "In the first place, he didn't ask me. And in the second, I didn't ask him. We were more comfortable being friends. Satisfied?"

"Maybe I'll beat him up anyway. On principle."

After setting his wine aside, he took her by the shoulders, turned her to face him. Even as she grinned at him, he pressed her back into the sink.

Hard, possessive, his mouth covered hers. The little purr that sounded in her throat enticed him to draw the kiss out, soften it, until all points of pleasure narrowed and centered just there.

When her head fell back in surrender, her hands slid limply down his arms, he eased back.

"That's so you remember which MacKade you're with now."

She had to remind herself to breathe. "What was your name again?"

He grinned, then closed his teeth over her sensitized bottom lip. "Tell you what. Why don't we skip necking on the couch and go try out the back seat of my car?"

"That's quite an offer." It was fascinating to feel her own head spin. "I think I'll take you up on it."

Rafe let himself into the Barlow house at midnight. He'd recognized the car at the top of the lane, and he wasn't surprised to find Jared in the parlor, brooding over a beer.

"Foreclosing already, Lawyer MacKade?"

Instead of rising to the bait, Jared stared down at his beer. "I put my house on the market today. Didn't feel like staying there."

Rafe grunted, sat down on his sleeping bag to pull off his boots. He knew the dark moods, often had them himself. Either he'd manage to shake Jared out of it, or they'd both ride through it.

"Never liked that house, no personality. Just like your ex-wife."

It was so cold, and so true, Jared had to laugh. "Decent investment, though. I'll make a profit."

Rafe shook his head at the beer Jared held out. "They don't taste the same without a smoke. Besides, I gotta be up in six and a half hours. I was going to come look for you," he added.

"Oh? Why?"

"To beat the hell out of you." With a yawn, Rafe lay back. "It'll have to wait till tomorrow. I'm too relaxed."

"Okay. Any particular reason?"

"You kissed my woman." Rafe figured he had just about enough energy to strip off his pants.

"I did?" Jared tossed his legs up over the settee. A slow smile curved his lips. "Oh, yeah. Oh, *yeah*..." he said again, with more feeling. "It's all coming back to me. When'd she get to be your woman?"

Rafe heaved his jeans aside, started on his shirt. "That's what comes from living in the city. You're out of the loop, bro. She's mine now."

"Does she know that?"

"*I* know." With his eyes closed, he dragged the sleeping bag over him. "I'm thinking about keeping her."

Jared choked on his beer. "You mean like a wife?"

"I mean like keeping her," Rafe repeated. No way was he going to try to get his tongue around a word like *wife*. "Keeping things the way they are now."

This was interesting, Jared mused. And even more fun than brooding. "And how are things now?"

"Things are good." Rafe could smell her on the quilted material of the sleeping bag. "I'm still going to have to break your face. It's the principle."

"Understood." Jared stretched out, settled back. "Then again, I never did pay you back for talking Sharilyn Bester, now Fenniman, into riding out to the quarry with you to skinny-dip."

"I was just easing her broken heart after you'd dumped her."

"Yeah. But it's the principle."

Considering, Rafe scratched his face. "You got a point. But Sharilyn, pretty as she is, is no Regan Bishop."

"I never got to see Regan naked."

"That's why you're still breathing." Rafe shifted, folded his arms under his head. "Maybe we'll call it even."

"I can sleep easy now."

Rafe's lips twitched at the dry tone. "I'm sorry about your house, Jared, if you are."

"I'm not sorry about it, really. It just brought a lot of things back. I screwed up as much as Barbara did, Rafe. It would have been easier if we'd yelled at each other, threw things." He took a last swig and set the empty bottle on the floor. "There's nothing more demoralizing than a civilized divorce between two people who couldn't care less about each other."

"It's got to be better than getting your heart broken."

"I don't know. I kind of wish I'd had the chance."

They were both silent as the sound of weeping drifted down the stairs.

"Ask her," Rafe suggested. "I'd bet she'd tell you you're better off."

"Maybe you should start thinking exorcism," Jake said, smiling at the idea as his eyes drooped and he settled himself for sleep.

"No. I like having them around. I've had plenty of time to be alone."

Chapter 9

It was rare for Rafe to dream. He preferred his fantasies during waking hours, so that his consciousness could appreciate them.

But he dreamed that night, as the fire burned low and the moon rose over drifts of snow, if you could call it a dream...

He was running, terror and smoke at his heels. His eyes were burning from fatigue, and from the horror he'd already seen.

Men blown apart before they could scream from the shock and agony. The ground exploding, hacked by mortar fire, drenched with blood. The smell of death was in his nostrils, and he knew he'd never be free of it.

Oh, and he longed for the scent of magnolias and roses, for the lush green hills and rich brown fields of his home. If he had had tears left, he would have wept them for the quiet gurgling of the river that wound through his family's plantation, the bright laughter of his sisters, the crooning songs of the field hands.

He was afraid, mortally afraid, that everything he'd known and treasured was already gone. His most desperate wish was to get back, to see it again.

He wanted to see his father again, to tell him his son had tried to be a man.

The battle raged everywhere. In the fields, through the corn, in his heart. So many of his comrades lay dead on these godforsaken rocky hills of Maryland.

He'd lost his way. He hadn't been able to see through the choking smoke, or hear through the thunder of guns and the horrible shrieks of men. Suddenly he was running, running as a coward runs for any hole to crawl in.

Mixed with the horror now was a shame just as terrible. He'd forgotten his duty, and lost his honor. Now, somehow, he must find them both again.

The woods were thick, carpeted with the dying leaves that fell, brilliant in golds and russets, from the trees. He had never been so far north, seen such color, or smelled the poignant decay of autumn.

He was only seventeen.

A movement ahead had him fumbling his rifle onto his shoulder. The blue uniform was all he could see, and he fired too quickly, and poorly. The answering shot had fire singeing his arm. Driven by pain and terror, he gave a wild Rebel yell and charged.

He wished he hadn't seen the eyes, the eyes of the enemy, as wide and terror-glazed and young as his own. Their bayonets crashed, point to point. He smelled the blood, and the stinking scent of fear.

He felt the steel of his blade slice into flesh, and his stomach roiled. He felt the rip of his own, and cried out in agony. He fought, blindly, bitterly, recklessly, until there was nothing inside him but the battle. And when they both lay in their own blood, he wondered why.

He was crawling, delirious with pain. He needed to get home for supper, he thought. Had to get home. There was the house, he could see it now. He dragged himself over rocks and dying summer flowers, leaving his blood staining the grass.

Hands were lifting him. Soft voices. He saw her standing over him, an angel. Her hair like a halo, her eyes warm, her voice filled with the music of the South he yearned for.

Her face was so beautiful, so gentle, so sad.

She stroked his head, held his hand, walking beside him as others carried him up curving steps.

I'm going home, he told her. *I have to go home.*

You'll be all right, she promised. *You'll go home as soon as you're well again.*

She looked away from him, up, and her lovely face went pale as a ghost's.

No. He's hurt. He's just a boy. Charles, you can't.

He saw the man, saw the gun, heard the words.

I'll have no Confederate scum in my house. No wife of mine will put her hands on a Rebel.

Rafe jolted awake with the sound of a gunshot ringing in his ears. He sat where he was while it echoed away, until all that was left was his brother's quiet breathing.

Chilled, he rose, added logs to the fire. Then he sat, watching the flames and waiting for dawn.

Regan slept like a baby. With the kids off to school and Cassie taking the early shift at the diner, she indulged herself with a second cup of coffee. She still prized her privacy, but she'd discovered she liked having the company.

It was nice having the children pad around the house in the morning, having Emma offer one of her solemn kisses or Connor one of his rare smiles.

She liked beating Cassie to the kitchen so that she could fix breakfast and smooth down pale, sleep-tousled hair.

Motherhood had never been one of her ambitions, but she was beginning to wonder if she wouldn't be good at it.

She picked up a crayon Emma had left on the table. She smelled it, and smiled. It was funny, she thought, how quickly a house could smell like children. Crayons and white paste, hot chocolate and soggy cereal.

And it was funny how quickly she'd come to look forward to finding them there after work.

Absently she tucked the crayon in her pocket. Work was exactly where she had to go.

Out of habit, she rinsed her coffee cup in the sink, set it on the drain. After a last glance around, she opened the door in the kitchen and headed down the stairs to open the shop for the day.

She'd barely turned the Open sign around, unlocked

the door and moved behind the counter to unlock the till when Joe Dolin walked in.

The quick spurt of alarm came first. Then she soothed it by reminding herself that he was here, and Cassie wasn't.

He'd put on weight even in the three years she'd known him. There was muscle there still, but it was cushioned by too many six-packs. She imagined he'd been an attractive man once, before his square face had bloated and his moody brown eyes had sunken behind bags.

He had a chipped front tooth she didn't know was courtesy of a younger Rafe's fist, and a nose that had been broken by Rafe, and several others.

With disgust, she remembered that he had tried, once or twice, to touch her. Had watched her, more than once or twice, with greedy eyes and a knowing smile.

Regan hadn't even told Cassie that. And never would.

She braced herself for the altercation, but he shut the door quietly, took off his billed cap and held it humbly in his hands, like a peasant before the queen.

"Regan. I'm sorry to bother you."

The penitent sound of his voice and bowed head almost softened her. But she remembered the bruises on Cassie's neck. "What do you want, Joe?"

"I heard Cassie's staying with you."

Just Cassie, she noted. Nothing about his children. "That's right."

"I guess you know about the trouble."

"Yes, I know. You beat her, and you were arrested."

"I was awful drunk."

"The court may find that an excuse. I don't."

His eyes narrowed and flashed, but he kept his head down. "I feel terrible about it. Done nothing but worry about her for days. Now they've fixed it so I can't even go near her to tell her so. I come to ask you a favor."

He lifted his head then, and his eyes were moist. "Cassie sets a lot of store by you."

"I set a lot of store by her," Regan said evenly. She would not let the sight of a man's tears blur her judgment.

"Yeah, well. I was hoping you'd talk to her for me. See that she gives me another chance. I can't ask her myself, long as there's that damn restraining order. But she'll listen to you."

"You're giving me credit for influence over Cassie I don't have, Joe."

"No, she'll listen to you," he insisted. "She's always running off at the mouth about how smart you are. You tell her to come on home, and she'll do it."

Very slowly, Regan placed her palms on the countertop. "If she'd listened to me, she would have left you years ago."

His unshaven jaw tightened. "Now, you look. A man's got a right—"

"To beat his wife?" she snapped. "Not in my book, he doesn't, and not in the law's. No, I won't tell her to come back to you, Joe. And if that's all you came in for, you'll have to leave."

His lips peeled back, showing clenched teeth, his eyes hardened like marbles. "Still all high-and-mighty. You think you're better than me."

"No, I don't. I *know* I'm better than you. Get out of my shop or I'll have Sheriff MacKade throw you in jail for harassment."

"A woman belongs to her husband." He crashed his fist on the counter, hard enough to have a crack splitting through the glass. "You tell her to get her skinny butt home, if she knows what's good for her. And what's good for you."

Fear trembled in Regan's throat, and was swallowed, hard. As if it were a talisman, she closed a hand around the crayon in her pocket. "Is that a threat?" she asked coolly. "I don't believe your parole officer would approve. Shall I call him and ask?"

"Bitch. You're nothing but a frigid, dried-up bitch who can't get herself a real man." He wanted to hit her, to feel his fist pound into that ice-queen face. "You get between me and my wife and both of you'll find out what it's like. When I finish with her, I'll come after you. We'll see if you're so high and mighty when I'm finished."

He jammed his hat back on his head, spun to the door. "You tell her what I said. You tell her I'm waiting. She'd better have that bastard MacKade tear up those papers and be home by suppertime."

The instant the door slammed behind him, Regan slumped against the counter. Her hands were shaking, and she hated it, hated being afraid, hated being vulnerable. She grabbed the phone, had nearly followed through on her first instinct to call Rafe when she stopped herself.

That was wrong, she thought, carefully replacing the receiver. For so many reasons it was wrong. Wouldn't his first reaction be to hunt Joe down, to fight? He'd probably get hurt and certainly more fighting wasn't going to solve anything.

She straightened and drew a few calming breaths. Where was her pride, her sense of control? She had always handled herself and any situation that came her way. Her feelings for Rafe shouldn't—couldn't change that intrinsic part of her. She wouldn't allow it. So, she would do what was right, what was practical, and what was necessary. Regan picked up the phone and dialed the sheriff's office.

"He was almost pitiful at first." The tea sloshed in her cup. With a grimace, Regan set it down again. "I guess he spooked me more than I'd thought."

"Shake all you want," Devin told her, and frowned at the crack in her counter. It could have been worse, he thought grimly. A lot worse. "I have to say, I didn't think he was fool enough to pull a stunt like this."

"I don't think he'd been drinking." Regan cleared her throat. "At least he wasn't drunk. He got steadily more angry, steadily more abusive." She reached for her tea again. "I don't have any witnesses. It was just him and me."

"You file charges, I'll go after him."

Her lips trembled upward. "It sounds like you're looking forward to it."

"You don't know the half of it."

"I'll file charges. Cassie?"

"I had one of my deputies go to the diner as soon as you called. He'll hang out there and get paid for drinking coffee and flirting with Ed. I've got another one driving by the school."

"The kids." Her blood ran cold. "You don't think he'd go after the kids?"

"No, I don't think he gives two damns about them."

"You're right." She tried to feel relieved. "He never said a word about them. Only Cassie. It was as if his children didn't exist. Well, I'll lock up and go with you now, if that's all right."

"The sooner the better. Odds are he's at home, knocking back a bottle and waiting for her."

Once the complaint was official, Regan detoured to the market. She had a feeling both she and Cassie were going to need a lift that evening. Comfort food was in order. Spaghetti and meatballs, she decided, and double-fudge brownies.

While she waited for her purchases to be bagged, she tried not to chuckle at the darting looks and whispers. The gossip brigade, she thought, was in full march.

Mrs. Metz, all two hundred and twenty pounds of her, waddled over. "Why, Regan Bishop, I thought that was you."

"Hello, Mrs. Metz." Here, Regan thought, was the brigade's head scout. "Do you think we're going to get hit with snow again?"

"Ice storm," she said with a shake of her head. "Heard on the radio. Into February now, and don't look like this winter's ever going to end. Surprised to see you in here this time of day."

"Business is slow." Regan counted out bills for the groceries. "Everybody's hibernating."

"Know what you mean. Still, you got yourself some business over at the old Barlow place, don't you?"

"Yes, indeed." Willing to play, Regan set the bag on her hip. "It's really coming along, too. It'll be a show-place when it's finished."

"Never thought to see the day anybody'd bother

fixing her up. Never thought to see Rafe MacKade come riding back into town, neither." Her curious eyes brightened. "Guess he did pretty well for himself down South."

"Apparently."

"You can't tell about those MacKade boys. They fool you every time. You know that Rafe crashed his daddy's Ford pickup on Marble Quarry Road before he so much as had a license. That was right after Buck died, as I recall. He was wild as wild can be, that Rafe. Chasing girls, picking fights, flying around on the back roads on that noisy motorcycle of his. Time was, when you found trouble, there was always a MacKade boy in the middle of it."

"Times change, I suppose."

"Not that much, they don't." Her chins wagged as she chuckled. "I seen him around town. He's still got that look in his eye. Little bird told me he had that eye on you."

"Well, your little bird's right. And I've got mine right back on him."

Mrs. Metz laughed so hard she had to put down her box of Ho-Hos to hold her belly. "With a boy like that, you'd better keep it there. He'd be harder to keep down than spit on a hot griddle. He was a bad one, Regan. Bad boys turn into dangerous men."

"I know." Regan winked. "That's why I like him. You come in and browse real soon, Mrs. Metz."

"I'll do that." Chuckling to herself, she emptied her cart. "Stop gawking, boy," she snapped at the skinny clerk, who was still watching Regan's retreat, "and ring me up here. You ain't never going to be dangerous enough to reel in that kind of woman."

Amused by the encounter, Regan strolled down the sidewalk. It was a good town, she thought, lifting a hand in response to a greeting from across the street. The sidewalks were uneven, heaved up by tree roots and frost, the library was only open three days a week, and the post office was closed for a full hour every afternoon.

But despite that, or perhaps because of it, it was a good town. She didn't think Rafe realized he'd been welcomed home.

No fatted calf, she mused, crossing at the corner and turning down Main. That wasn't their style. The prodigal son just slipped back into the town's rhythm with neither a hitch nor fanfare.

When he left again, his departure would be just as

unheralded. A few comments over the counter at the post office, some speculation at the diner. Then the town would move along, as easy as ever.

She hoped she would.

Shifting her bag, she circled around the side of the shop. Enjoy the moment, she reminded herself. Don't project into the future. Those were the rules; she'd stated them herself. All she had to do was follow them.

And if she found an excuse to slip by his house later, steal an hour with him, so much the better.

Bolstered by the idea, she took her keys from her pocket. She jingled them as she climbed the stairs with her groceries.

If she'd been paying attention, if she hadn't been thinking about Rafe, perhaps she would have noticed sooner. But her hand was already reaching for the door when she saw that it wasn't on its hinges, but was propped there.

Her mind stayed blank for an instant too long.

Even as she spun around to run, Joe hauled the door aside. The crash dragged a shriek from her. It was choked off to a gurgle when his arm jerked around her neck.

"Wondered which one of you'd come first. This is

good." His breath panted out, sour with whiskey and excitement. "Been wanting to get my hands on you for a long time."

He pressed his mouth to her ear, excited by the way she tried to curl away from him. "I'm going to show you what a real man's all about. Going to get you out of those prim and proper clothes and show you real good."

He panted as his free hand came around to squeeze hard on her breast. Her skin crawled, and for one hideous moment the fear was so bright it blinded her eyes, and her reason.

"I'm going to get me some of what I hear that bastard Rafe MacKade's been getting. Then I'm going to fix your face so nobody thinks it's so pretty anymore."

As he started to drag her over the broken door and inside, the horror of what he would do flashed through her. She swung back. Groceries flew, smashing into the little alley below. Her heels skidded back over the door.

"Cassie gets here, I'm going to give her the same. But first I'm going to enjoy taking you down a few pegs." With his free hand, he yanked her hair, darkly pleased when she whimpered.

Then she remembered the keys that were still gripped in her frozen fist. With prayers screaming in her head, she flung her hand back, hacking with the point she'd pushed between her clenched fingers.

He howled like a wild dog, and the vicious grip released. Dragging in air, she flew down the steps, certain he would be on her again in an instant. At the bottom, she stumbled, went down hard on her hands and knees. Prepared to scream, she looked back.

And saw him crumpled on the landing, holding a hand to his face, while blood dripped through his fingers. Like a woman in a trance, she rose to her feet, put one foot slowly in front of the other until she reached the diner. The buzzing in her ears warned her to take deep, careful breaths.

She stepped inside, closed the door behind her, unaware that her coat was hanging by one sleeve and the knees of her slacks were torn and bloody.

Cassie dropped the tray she was holding, shattering dishes. "Regan! My God!"

"I think you should call Devin," Regan said, testing each word as she spoke it. "Joe's on the landing of my apartment. I think I hurt him." When the room revolved, she braced a hand on the back of a booth. "I have to sit down now."

"Go call Devin," Ed snapped, and rushed over to ease Regan into a booth. "Head down." In a quick movement, she had Regan's head between her knees. "Long, deep breaths, that's a girl." Eyes sharp, she scanned the room, where a half a dozen customers sat staring. "Well, what are you waiting for? One of you big strong men get on over there and hold that son of a bitch for the sheriff. You, Horace, get up off your lard butt and get this girl a glass of water."

Ed's rasped orders had everyone moving at once. Satisfied, she eased Regan up again. "Got a little color back," she declared, and sat back on her haunches. She took a cigarette from the pack in her apron pocket, lit it with a wooden match. After one long drag, she smiled. "Hope to hell you hurt him bad, honey. Real bad."

Sitting in Devin's office, with the coffee Shane had poured for her warming her hands, Regan was sure she was over the worst of it. Everything had happened too fast for anything but pure emotion. But the rabbity fear had passed now, and she could think.

Beside her, Cassie sat saying nothing. Shane paced,

like a boxer revving up for a match. At his desk, Devin coolly filled out a report.

"I'm sorry to ask you to go through it again, Regan," he began. "The clearer your statement, the easier it'll be to close it all up."

"That's all right. I'm fine now, really." Absently she picked at her torn slacks. The knees beneath still burned. As much, she thought, from Ed's liberal application of antiseptic as from their abrupt meeting with asphalt. "I'd like to get it over with. I can—"

She broke off when the door burst open. For an instant, she saw nothing but Rafe's face—pale, hard as rock, lit with eyes green enough, sharp enough, to murder in one vicious slice.

The rabbit pulse pounded in her throat. Before she could get to her feet, he was on her, dragging her up, crushing her in an embrace that bruised ribs.

"You're all right? Are you hurt?" His voice was raw, brittle as broken glass. He couldn't think. There'd been nothing inside him but bright terror from the moment he got word of the attack. His body was ice, enveloping hers as he buried his face in her hair.

Perhaps that was why she began to tremble helplessly. "I'm okay. Really, I'm—" But her voice shuddered off. If she could have burrowed inside him, she would have.

"Did he hurt you?" With a hand he was fighting to steady, he stroked her hair, eased her face back so that he could see for himself. "Did he touch you?"

She could only shake her head and press her face against his shoulder.

With his arms tight, as possessive as they were protective, he stared at Devin over Regan's head. His eyes fired like torches. "Where is he?"

"He's in custody."

Rafe's gaze whipped toward the cells in the back.

"He's not here, Rafe." Though his voice was calm, Devin was braced for the attack. "You're not going to be able to get to him."

"You think you can stop me?"

From behind, where he'd stood since he'd followed Rafe in, Jared laid a hand on his brother's shoulder. "Why don't you sit down?"

With a snarl humming in his throat, Rafe jerked the restraining hand aside. "Back off."

"This is the law's problem now," Devin told him, rising slowly.

"The hell with the law, and you with it. I want to know where he is."

"You find him, Rafe, I'll hold your coat." Primed for action, Shane smiled thinly. "If you had a coat. Always hated the son of a bitch."

"Shut up," Jared muttered, glancing down at the silent Cassie.

"You can stick your lawyer talk," Shane told him, fists already bunched. "I'm with Rafe on this."

"I don't need you or anybody else with me. Don't get in my way, Devin."

"I'm already in your way. Now sit down, or I'll throw your ass in a cell."

He moved so fast, Regan had time only to squeak while Rafe lunged over the desk and had Devin by the shirtfront. She'd never considered herself sheltered, but the things they shouted at each other, the echo of the sentiments from the two MacKades behind her, had her already shocked system shuddering.

There was no doubt in her mind that blood would flow any moment.

"Stop it," she said, but the order was shaky and weak under the vicious words hurling through the room. "I said stop it," she repeated, hugging herself.

Something crashed behind her, and shot her pulse to critical. "Stop it this minute!" she bellowed.

The surprising power in her voice halted Rafe's fist and put a stop to the shoving match behind her. Four hard-eyed men stared at her, like statues frozen in battle.

"You're acting like children. *Worse* than children. What good is it going to do anyone for the four of you to punch each other out? It's just typical," she said, more disgusted now than frightened. "Just the sort of typical behavior I'd expect from a bunch of boneheaded baboons. Real heroes." With a sniff, she grabbed her coat. "Well, I'm certainly not going to stand here and watch the four of you beat one another to a pulp."

"Sit down, Regan." When she continued toward the door, Rafe swore and went after her. "Sit down," he repeated, holding back his rage and turning her gently. "God, look at your hands."

Shaken all over again, he gathered them carefully in his, pressed his lips to the abraded palms. It was a gesture that had the remaining MacKades shifting in embarrassment.

"What do you expect me to do?" The rest of the

anger drained and left him helpless. "What do you expect me to feel?"

"I don't know." She no longer knew exactly what she was feeling herself, not with those eyes so concentrated on her face. "I just want to get this over with, Rafe. Please, let me tell Devin what he needs to know, so I can get this over with."

"Fine." He let her go, stepped back. "Do what you have to do."

She walked back to her chair, accepted the fresh mug Jared offered. Devin questioned, she answered. Rafe listened. Then he left, without a word.

She tried not to be hurt by it, tried to understand it. "Devin, can you tell me what to expect now?"

"My deputy will call in once they're finished with Joe at the hospital. He'll be transferred. He broke parole, and the restraining order, so he'll serve his full time on the earlier charges."

It was a small satisfaction, Devin thought with a quick look at Cassie. She hadn't moved or spoken in thirty minutes.

"Now he'll face additional charges," Devin went on. "Breaking and entering, assault, attempted rape.

We'll toss in the property damage. There may be a trial, and you'd have to testify."

"I'm prepared for that."

"Under the circumstances, his lawyer may advise him to deal and plead guilty."

At Devin's questioning glance, Jared nodded. "That's what I'd do."

"Yeah, well." It was hard not to hate the system, Devin mused, when it got personal. "Either way, he's going away for a good while. I figure three to five. He won't be bothering you again. Either of you."

"Well, then." Regan drew in a deep breath. "It's done. Cassie and I can go home now?"

"Sure. I'll be in touch."

"I can't go home with you." For the first time since she'd come into the office, Cassie tried her voice. It was small and rusty.

"Of course you can."

"How can I?" She stared at the lovely smoke gray slacks Regan wore, at the nasty tears in the soft material. "How could you even want me after what he's done to you?"

"What *he's* done," Regan said quietly. "Not you, Cassie. You're not responsible."

"Of course I am." It cost Cassie to lift her head, to look into Regan's eyes. "I know what he might have done to you if you hadn't been strong enough to stop him. Done to you to get to me, Regan. You're the best friend I've ever had."

"Then let me keep being your friend."

"I want that, and I know you've already forgiven me."

"Cassie, there's nothing to forgive. Don't take this on," Regan murmured, covering Cassie's hands with hers.

"I have to, because I have to start figuring out how to forgive myself now. I'm going to start by taking my kids home and finding a way to make the kind of life for them they deserve. I need to start taking care of myself and them. I need to do that."

"In a few more days," Regan protested.

"No, now." She closed her eyes, steadied herself, then opened them and looked at Jared. "Can you help me, Jared?"

"Of course I can. Whatever you need, honey. There are plenty of programs—"

"No." She pressed her lips together hard. It was time, she told herself, long past time, that she took a stand. "I want to file for divorce. Today. I need you to tell me what to do."

"All right." He took her hand to help her up, then slipped an arm gently around her shoulders. "Why don't you come with me now? We'll take care of everything."

"'Bout time," Shane muttered, the minute the door closed behind them. He shrugged at the blazing look Devin aimed at him. "Hey, we all know she should have ditched that bastard years ago."

"You won't get any argument there." Regan rose, surprised she wasn't as steady as she'd believed. "But that was hard for her. It's going to be hard for her to follow through."

"She wouldn't have done it if he hadn't hurt somebody else," Devin mumbled. "That's the kind of thing it would take for her."

"Then I'm glad he did. And I'm glad I hurt him right back." Regan took a deep breath, then asked the question that had been hovering in a corner of her mind. "His eye, Devin?"

"I can let you know when I find out. If you want me to."

"I think I have to know." She held out a hand for

his, not to shake, but to hold. "You've been wonderful. I know Rafe was upset, but he was wrong in the things he said to you. You did everything you could. You did everything right."

"If I'd done everything right, it wouldn't have happened."

"You know better than that." She squeezed, then winced as her hand throbbed. "I'm going home, take a bottle of aspirin, and crawl into bed for a few hours. Please call when you hear anything."

"I will. Shane?"

"Ahead of you, like always." He already had Regan's coat, and he helped her into it. "I'll drive you home and fix that door for you."

"Thanks." With a smile, she kissed his cheek. "Baboons or not, the MacKade brothers aren't half-bad."

"Baby—" he put an arm around her waist to lead her out "—we're all bad. Later, Dev." When he'd helped her into his truck, he paused. "Rafe'll come around. He just needs to go punch something."

"That's the answer?"

"Hey, it works." He slammed her door, then circled the truck to climb behind the wheel.

"You'd have gone with him. After Joe."

"We'd have all gone with him." Shane glanced in the rearview, then whipped the truck into a quick and illegal U-turn. "Dev and Jared would have spouted off for a while about law and order. We'd have shoved each other around. Then we'd have gone with him." With some regret, he shook his head. "It would've been fun."

"Fun." She could almost laugh as she let her head sink back on the seat.

"Nobody messes with a MacKade woman."

"Oh, really? And is that my status at this point?"

He caught the tone, and then, with a wary glance, the martial look in her eyes. "I just meant…seeing as you and Rafe… That is, the way he's…" Even a MacKade knew the value of retreat. "I ain't touching this one."

He pulled up at the base of her stairs and looked up to study the door. "Looks like somebody beat me to it."

"What?" She was still simmering.

"I'll check it, but it looks from here like it's already been fixed." He got out of the truck, climbed the stairs. "Yep. Few nicks and scratches, but it's back on its hinges." As a precaution, he tried the lock, gave it a good shove. "Solid. Rafe probably took care of it."

"I see." It did nothing to appease her. "I'll have to be sure to thank him, won't I?"

"Yeah." Shane retreated again, backing down the stairs. "Are you going to be all right? Want me to get you anything, or hang around?"

"No, no, I'm fine. Just fine." It wasn't pleasant to take out her keys, but she did it, turned the lock. "I appreciate the ride."

"No problem." As he hurried back to his truck, Shane decided Rafe had a problem. A big one. It gave him a reason to smile all the way through town.

Chapter 10

It felt good to beat on something. Even if it was only a nail. To prevent himself beating on something, or someone else, Rafe had closed himself inside the east-wing bedroom. The look in his eye had warned any and all of his men to keep their distance—if they wanted to keep their teeth.

The sounds of construction bumped against the walls, a sound just violent enough to suit his black mood. Rafe ignored the nail gun at his disposal and beat in nails with hammer and muscle. Every new stud that he secured with nails and a swing of his arm was Joe Dolin's face.

When the door opened behind him, Rafe bared his teeth without looking around. "Get the hell out. Stay out or you're fired."

"Go ahead and fire me." Regan slammed the door at her back. "Then I can say what I have to say to you without damaging our professional relationship."

He looked over his shoulder now, briefly. She'd changed, he noted. Not just the slacks, but everything—shirt, blazer, jewelry. From her hair to her shoes, she was neat as a pin.

But he remembered exactly how she'd looked, frazzled, pale, with blood on her clothes.

"You don't want to be here right now." He set another nail, shot it home.

"You couldn't be more accurate on that, MacKade, but I'm here."

She'd had to shower first, had to scrub herself everywhere and throw out every stitch she'd been wearing when Joe touched her. But she was steady again, and ready to deal with Rafe MacKade.

"I want to know what the hell is wrong with you."

If he told her, she was liable to laugh in his face. And that, he was dead sure, would push him over that final edge.

"I'm busy, Regan. Weather's cost me a full day."

"Don't hand me that. Look at me when I'm talking to you, damn it." When he didn't, just kept battering nails into wood, she fisted her hands on her hips. "Why did you leave Devin's office that way? Just leave?"

"I had things to do."

To illustrate her opinion of that, she kicked at a toolbox. "I suppose I'm to thank you now for fixing my door."

"I'll bill you."

"Why are you mad at me?" she demanded. "I didn't do anything to—"

Her breath sucked in as the hammer sailed across the room and crashed into a newly framed wall.

"No, you didn't do a damn thing. You just got yourself tossed around, bruised, bloodied up and damn near raped. Why the hell should that bother me?"

Someone had to be calm, she told herself. Obviously, the way his eyes were glowing, it was going to have to be her. "I know you're upset about what happened."

"Yeah, I'm upset." He picked up the toolbox, heaved it, because it made more sense than throwing her around. Metal and steel crashed and scattered like small bombs. "I'm just a little upset. Now get out."

"I won't." Instead she angled her chin. "Go ahead, big guy, throw something else. When you've got it out of your system, we'll have a civilized conversation."

"You'd better get it through that thick head that there's nothing civilized about me."

"Oh, that's coming through loud and clear," she tossed back. "What's next? You want to take a shot at me? That should prove you're a bigger man than Joe Dolin."

His eyes went black. For an instant, a heartbeat, she thought she saw hurt mixed with the rage. And it shamed her. "I'm sorry." Fumbling, she lifted her hands. "You didn't deserve that. I didn't mean that."

Now there was only rage, viciously controlled. "You usually say what you mean." He held up a hand before she could speak again. "You want to have a conversation, fine. We'll have a damn conversation."

He strode to the door, simmering when she flinched. Yanking it open, he bellowed to every corner of the rambling house. "Out! Everybody out, now!"

He slammed the door again, satisfied by the scramble of feet and the clatter of tools.

"There's no need for the work to stop," she began. "I'm sure this will only take a few minutes."

"Sometimes it just can't be your way."

"I don't know what you mean."

"No, I don't guess you do." Disgusted, he hauled open the door again. "Somebody give me a damn cigarette," he shouted. But as there was no one brave enough to approach, he ended up slamming the door again.

Regan watched, quietly fascinated, while he paced and swore. His shirt was shoved up to the elbows, a tool belt was slung at his hips like a holster. He'd wrapped a bandanna around his forehead to catch the sweat. He looked, she thought, like a bandit who would just as soon kill as steal.

And it was certainly ridiculous to be aroused.

"I could make coffee," she began, then let out a breath at the razor-edged look he shot her. "Maybe not. Rafe—"

"Just shut up."

Her back jammed straight as a poker. "I don't care to be spoken to that way."

"Get used to it. I've held back long enough with you."

"Held back?" Her eyes went wide. If he hadn't

looked like a maniac, she might have laughed. "You've been holding back? I'd like to see what you consider cutting loose."

"You're about to." He gnawed off the words like stringy meat from a bone. "You're ticked off that I left? Well, now you're going to be treated to what would have happened if I'd stayed."

"Don't you touch me." Her arms shot up, hands fisted like those of a boxer ready to spar. "Don't you dare."

Eyes simmering, he closed a hand over her fist and used his leverage to push her back to the door. "Same goes, darling. I gave you a chance to walk, you didn't take it."

"Don't call me darling in that tone of voice."

The way his lips peeled back, she wouldn't have been surprised to see fangs. "God, you're a piece of work." He tossed her hand down and walked away, because it was safer for both of them. "You want to know why I left. That's the big, burning question, isn't it? That's what had you coming over here? Coming to me?"

"Yes."

"But you didn't come to me this morning when he

threatened you. You didn't come to me when he hurt you." And that, Rafe thought, however it devastated him, was that.

"I had to tell Devin," she began.

"Yeah. You had to tell Devin." Bitterly calm now, he turned back. "You know what I heard in that nice and detailed statement you made, Regan? Dolin came into your place this morning, just like I thought he would."

"And I handled it," she countered. "Just like I told you I would."

"Sure, you're great at handling things. He threatened you. He scared you."

"Yes, all right, he scared me." And she was scared now, too, she realized, of where this was leading. "That's why I called Devin."

"But not me. You went down to Devin's office, filed your charges."

"Yes, of course. I wanted Joe arrested."

"Nice and tidy. Then you went *grocery* shopping."

"I…" She linked her hands together, pulled them apart. "I thought—I knew Cassie was going to be upset, and I wanted… I just thought if I fixed a meal it would make us both feel better."

"And in all that time, going to Devin's, to the market, walking there and back, you never stopped to call me. It never even occurred to you, did it?"

"I was—" She opened her mouth, closed it again. "All right, yes. It was my first reaction, but I calmed down and decided against it."

"You calmed down?"

"Yes, I realized it was my problem, and my responsibility to handle it."

Her simple honesty sliced through him like a blade. He could almost see himself split in half, one part rage, one part misery. "And after he had you, after he had his hands on you, and hurt you, tried to—"

He couldn't say it. If he did, he'd fall to pieces.

"You didn't think to call me then, either. I only heard it from Shane because he was in with Devin when the call came through, and he figured I'd be interested."

Somehow, she realized, she *had* hurt him. She'd never meant to. Hadn't known he could be hurt. "Rafe, I wasn't thinking at all." She started forward, stopped, knowing it would do no good to go farther. "I was numb. By the time I could really think again, I was in Devin's office. It all happened so fast," she said hurriedly, desperate now to make him see. To understand. "And part of the time it seemed as if I wasn't really there at all."

"You were handling it."

"I had to. It wouldn't have done any good to fall apart."

"You're real good at keeping yourself together." He walked over, picked up the hammer. "All by yourself."

"I have to be. I expect myself to be, because—"

"You don't want to be like your mother," he finished for her.

It sounded so callous, and so foolish. "All right, yes, that's partially true. It's important for me to be a certain way, but that really doesn't apply to this. If I didn't call you, it was only because…"

"You didn't need me." His eyes were level, and no longer hot. He had very little heat left inside him. "You don't need me."

A new kind of panic was twisting through her. "That's not true."

"Oh, the sex is great." He smiled then, coolly, humoressly. "That's a need we handle together real well. It's my problem that I let it get personal. I won't make the mistake again."

"It's not about sex."

"Sure it is." He plucked a nail out of his pouch, set it in place. "It's been about sex right from the get-go. That's all we've got. It's plenty." He rammed the nail home. "You know where to find me when you've got the itch."

The blood drained from her cheeks and froze around her heart. "That's a horrible thing to say."

"Your rules, darling. Why complicate a good thing, right?"

"I don't want things to be this way between us, Rafe."

"Well, now I do. Take it or leave it." He rammed another nail into wood. She wasn't going to get the chance to hurt him again, he told himself. No woman hurt him like this.

She opened her mouth, primed to tell him she'd leave it. Leave him. And couldn't. Tears burned in her eyes, in her throat. Could there have been a worse possible time, she wondered, for her to realize she was in love with him?

"Is that the way you really feel?"

"I try to say what I mean, too."

Unwilling to humiliate herself, she swallowed the

tears. "And all this is because you're angry about what happened. About how I dealt with it."

"Let's just say it made everything clear. You don't want to clutter up your life, right?"

"No, I—"

"Hell, neither do I. Call it ego— I've got one. I didn't like you running to my brother instead of me. Like you said, I've got it out of my system. We can just go back to the way things were. The way things are."

She hadn't realized how much she could prefer that lethal temper over this calculated disinterest. "I'm not sure that's possible. I can't give you an answer right at the moment."

"You mull it over, Regan. You do that real well, too."

"Would you rather—" She pressed a hand to her lips, waited until she could steady her voice. "If you'd rather suspend our business relationship, I can give you the names of some other dealers in the area."

"No reason for that. I'm already behind." When he turned to her, all he saw was that her eyes were dry, her face was composed. "I can take shipment on this room in about a week, if you've got a problem with storage."

"That'll be fine. I'll make the arrangements." She

turned and reached blindly for the doorknob. Terrified she'd crumble, she walked away quickly. She didn't start to run until she was outside, with the wind slapping her wet cheeks.

When he heard the door close below, Rafe sat down on the floor. At the sound of weeping shimmering in the air, he rubbed his hands hard over his face.

"I know just how you feel," he muttered.

It was the first time in his checkered career that anyone had managed to break his heart. His only solace was that he'd make damn sure it was the last.

The predicted ice storm raged through, glazing the snow, turning the streets to glass. It was days before the temperature inched up enough to soften it. Each night the thermometer would plunge again, hardening and slickening every coated surface.

It didn't mean a damn thing to Rafe. The lousy weather gave him an excuse to stay just where he was, work twenty out of every twenty-four hours. With every nail he hammered, every wall he sanded, the house became more his.

When he couldn't sleep, even after exhausting himself, he wandered the house with the other ghosts.

He was too busy to think about Regan. Or so he tried to convince himself.

Whenever he did, whenever she snuck through his well-fortified defenses, he just worked harder, longer.

"You look a little ragged, pal." Devin lit a cigarette and watched Rafe hammer freshly painted baseboard into place. "Remember that book—*Dorian Gray?* The way it's starting to look, you're the picture in the closet, and this house is old Dorian."

"Pick up a hammer, or beat it."

Instead, Devin crouched, ran a fingertip over the wide, carved trim. "Sure is pretty as a picture. What'd you call this color?"

"Rose dust." He framed the words like a dare.

"Yep, sure is pretty." Devin used an empty coffee can as an ashtray. "If you're into pink."

Rafe spared him a look. "You trying to start something?"

"Nope, just making conversation. They transferred Joe from the hospital today."

Rafe's eyes iced over before he turned away. "None of my business."

"He didn't lose his eye," Devin went on easily. "Be

wearing a patch for a while though. They can't tell yet if there'll be permanent damage."

"She should have aimed between his legs."

"Yeah, too bad about that. Well, I thought you'd want to know, he pleaded guilty to the B and E, the assault, on advice of counsel. They dumped the attempted rape charges to get the guilty plea and avoid trial, but he's not going to pass Go."

Rafe didn't want to care. "How long?"

"My guess is three, solid. Before you say it's not enough, I'm going to the sentencing tomorrow myself, and adding weight. When he's up for parole, in a year or so, I'll go back and add more."

"I said it's none of my business." Rafe toed in the last piece of baseboard. "How's Cassie holding up?"

"Okay, I guess. Jared's pushing through the divorce. With the spousal abuse and adultery, it won't take the usual year. Joe's not in much of a position to contest it. The quicker it's done, the quicker she and the kids can get on with things."

Thoughtfully he tapped his cigarette out in the can. "Aren't you going to ask how Regan's holding up?"

"No."

"Well, I'll tell you." Ignoring Rafe's snarl, Devin

folded his legs and sat. "She doesn't look like she's been getting a lot of sleep, if you ask me."

"I didn't."

"Ed says she hasn't been coming in for lunch, so I guess her appetite's off, too. I could figure that experience with Joe shook her up enough to interfere with her sleeping and eating. But I got a hunch it's something else."

"She'll handle it. She's good at taking care of herself."

"Good thing, too. Odds are, if Joe had managed to drag her inside that day, somebody would've seen the door quick enough, heard the ruckus. Still, he could've done a lot of damage in a short time."

"Don't you think I know that?" Rafe shot out. "Do you think I don't know what he could have done to her?"

"Yeah, I think you know it. I think it's eating at you, and I'm sorry. Are you ready to listen to me?"

"No."

But there wasn't any heat behind the denial, so Devin prepared to say his piece. "Witnesses in the diner said they thought she was drunk at first when she came in, the way she was walking. She'd have passed out if Ed hadn't gotten her down first."

"I don't need to hear this."

"Yeah," Devin murmured, watching Rafe's knuckles whiten on the hilt of the hammer, "you do. When I got to her, Rafe, she was in shock. Are you getting this? Her pupils were as narrow as the point of one of those nails. I was set to have her taken into Emergency, but she pulled herself together. I watched her do it. It was impressive."

"So she's tough." The image projecting into his mind scraped him raw. "Tell me something I don't know."

"Okay. I don't figure you were in any shape to see the way she looked at you when you walked into my office. She'd pulled herself together because she had to, because that's the way she's made, I guess. Then you walked in. A man could go his whole life without having a woman look at him the way she looked at you."

"She doesn't need me."

"That's bull. You may be stupid, but you should know that."

"I know I was stupid enough to let her matter. To

let what she thought of me, what she wanted from me, matter. I'm not doing it again." He rose, hooked his hammer in his tool belt. "I don't need her, either."

With a sigh, Devin unfolded himself and stood. "You're cross-eyed in love with her."

"No, I'm not. I got soft on her for a while, then I got over it."

Devin pursed his lips. There was one quick, potentially painful way to handle this. "You're sure?"

"I just said so, didn't I?"

"Good." Devin smiled. "That clears the way. When I thought you had a thing for her, I didn't want to muscle in. Since you don't, I'll go see if I can...stimulate her appetite."

He was expecting the punch, and took the fist on the jaw philosophically. It was always satisfying to make a point. He lifted a hand, wiggled his jaw, mildly relieved it wasn't broken.

"Yeah, I can see how you got over it."

"I ought to hit you again," Rafe said between his teeth. It was infuriating, humiliating, to know how neatly he'd been conned.

"I wouldn't. That one was free." Cautious, Devin moved his jaw again. "Damn, Rafe, you've still got a nice right jab."

Almost amused, Rafe flexed his aching fingers. "You've still got a face like a rock. You son of a bitch."

"I love you, too." Cheered, Devin draped an arm over his brother's shoulders. "Feel better now?"

"No." Then he paused. "Maybe."

"You want to go find her and straighten this mess out?"

"I'm not crawling after some woman," Rafe mumbled.

You will, Devin thought. Sooner or later. "Well then, I got the night off. Want to get drunk and disorderly?"

"Yeah." They walked into the hall, started down the steps. "Why don't I meet you at the tavern? Ten o'clock."

"Suits me. I'll see if I can round up Shane and Jared."

"Just like old times. When Duff sees us coming, it'll scare the—" Rafe broke off, felt his heart skip. Regan stood straight-backed and cool-eyed at the base of the stairs.

"I've got your delivery." She'd worked very hard on being able to speak without inflection. "Your message said you'd be ready for it by three."

"Just." His stomach quivered, infuriating him. "You can have it hauled up."

"All right. Hello, Devin."

"Hello, Regan. I'm just on my way out. See you tonight, Rafe."

"Yeah." Rafe kept his eyes on Regan's as he came down the last few steps. "Have any trouble on the roads?"

"No. They're mostly clear now." She wondered that he couldn't see her heart bleeding. "I was able to get that feather mattress you wanted for the four-poster. I'll be happy to set it up so you can be sure you want to go with it."

"Appreciate it. I'll get out of your way. I've got—" Nothing, he realized. He had nothing. "Work," he said finally. "Give a yell when you're ready. I'll have your check."

She wanted to say something, anything, but he was already walking away. Squaring her shoulders, she went back to the door to instruct the movers.

It was nearly five when she finished arranging things exactly as she wanted them. She hadn't noticed the quiet that drifted in to replace the steady bang and buzz of labor. But as the light changed, she switched on the rose-patterned globe lamp by the button-backed chair she'd angled toward the fireplace.

There was no mantel there yet, no flames crackling. Faintly the scent of paint stirred in the air. But she thought the room was waiting to be lived in.

And the scent of roses hung like tears in the air.

A wedding-ring quilt, she mused, running her hand over one of the posts of the bed. A few pillows edged with lace to match the canopy that would drape overhead. A cedar chest, a hope chest, at the foot of the bed, filled with sweet-smelling linens and net bags of lavender sachet.

Yes, she thought, those would be just the right touches to finish it off. Perhaps some Irish lace at the windows, a silver-backed brush for the vanity.

It would be beautiful. It would be perfect.

She wished to God she'd never seen the room, the house, or Rafe MacKade.

He stood in the doorway, saying nothing, watching her move through the room, as graceful as any ghost.

Then her back stiffened. She turned and faced him.

Seconds passed, though it could have been eons for both of them.

"I was just finishing up," she managed to say.

"So I see." He stayed where he was, tore his gaze from hers and scanned the room. "It looks terrific."

"I have some tintypes and antique silver frames. I think they'd add a nice touch to the mantel when it's in place."

"Great."

The strain of manners was tearing at her stomach. "I noticed you've made a lot of progress on the next bedroom."

"It's coming along. I've got a couple more ready for drywall."

"You work fast."

"Yeah, that's what they always say." He pulled a check out of his pocket, stepped forward. "Payment on delivery."

"Thank you." Very deliberately, she opened the purse she'd set on a table, slipped the check inside. And damned him to hell. "I'll be going, then," she said briskly. She turned back and bumped solidly into him. "Excuse me." She took a step around. He shifted, blocked her. Made her heart pound like a drum. "You're in my way."

"That's right." And since he was, he took a good long look. "You look lousy."

"Thank you so much."

"You've got shadows under your eyes."

So much for cosmetics, she thought in disgust. "It's been a long day. I'm tired."

"How come you haven't been eating over at Ed's?"

She wondered why she'd ever thought she liked small towns. "Despite what you and the Antietam grapevine might think, what I do on my lunch hour is my business."

"Dolin's locked up. He's not going to bother you again."

"I'm not afraid of Joe Dolin." She tossed back her hair, proud of her own bravado. "I'm thinking about buying a gun."

"Think again."

She hadn't really thought of it the first time, but it grated to have him dictate to her. "That's right, you're the only one who can defend himself, or anyone else. Back off, MacKade. I'm finished here."

When he grabbed her arm, she swung out without

thinking. Her hand cracked against his cheek before she could stop it. Appalled, she stumbled back.

"Now look what you've made me do." Enraged and close to tears, she tossed down her purse. "I can't believe you goaded me into that. I've never struck anyone in my life."

"You did a pretty good job on your debut." Watching her, he ran his tongue over the inside of his stinging cheek. "You want to put your shoulder into it next time. Not much of a crack if you swing from the wrist."

"There won't be a next time. Unlike you, I don't have to hit people to make a point." She took a steadying breath. "I apologize."

"If you head for the door again, I'm going to get in your way again, and we're going to start this all over."

"All right." She left her purse where it lay. "Obviously there's something you want to say."

"If you keep aiming that chin at me, you're going to make me mad. I'm being civilized, asking how you are. Civilized is how you like it, isn't it?"

"I'm fine." She bit the words off. "And how are you?"

"Good enough. You want some coffee, a beer?"

"No, thank you so much." Who the hell was this man, she thought, making uselessly polite conversation while her insides tangled into dozens of frayed knots? "I don't want coffee or beer."

"What do you want, Regan?"

Now she recognized him. It took only that sharp, impatient tone to bring him back. And to make her yearn. "I want you to leave me alone."

He said nothing at all, just stepped out of her way.

Once more she picked up her purse. Once more she set it down again. "That's not true." The hell with her pride, with sense, even with her heart. It couldn't be any more battered than it already was.

"You'd never have made it to the door," he said quietly. "You probably knew that."

"I don't know anything except I'm tired of fighting with you."

"I'm not fighting. I'm waiting."

She nodded, sure she understood. If it was all he was willing to give her now, she would accept that. And she would make it enough. She stepped out of her shoes, unbuttoned her blazer.

"What are you doing?"

"Answering your ultimatum of last week." She tossed the blazer on the chair and unbuttoned her blouse. "You said take it or leave it. I'm taking it."

Chapter 11

It was a curve he hadn't been expecting. By the time he could speak, she was wearing nothing but two scraps of black silk. And all the blood had drained out of his head.

"Just like that?"

"It was always just like that, wasn't it, Rafe? Chemistry, pure and simple?"

He'd want her, she promised herself. By God, when she was done with him, he'd never stop wanting her. Keeping her eyes locked on his, she walked slowly toward him.

"Take it or leave it, MacKade." She put her hands

on his shirt and stunned them both by ripping it open and sending buttons flying. "Because I'm about to take you."

Her mouth was fire on his, burning, flashing, shooting dozens of wild blazes into him. Rocked to the core, he gripped her hips, fingers digging through silk to flesh.

"Put your hands on me." She sank her teeth into his shoulder. "I want your hands on me." Hers were dragging at his jeans, closing around him.

"Wait." But the bombs erupting inside him drowned out everything but pulsing, grappling need. With only his wounded heart as a pitiful weapon, he was defenseless against the spear thrust of desire. Against her.

He kicked himself free of clothes, lifted her off the floor.

He was deep inside her before they fell onto the bed.

It was all sweat and speed and blind sex. The hard slap of flesh against flesh, the raspy gasps of labored breathing. Teeth and nails and tangled tongues drove them both over the sumptuous mattress, rolling and riding.

It was a battle both had already surrendered to. Hot and hard and hurried, fast and frenzied and frantic, they pounded together. Wanting more, accepting less. The scent of roses choked the air with strong, sad perfume.

She straddled him, bowed back as his hands streaked over her. She wanted him to take her to that tenuous edge between pleasure and pain. There she would be alive, as she hadn't been since he'd turned from her.

She had to know that here, at least here, he was as helpless as she, as unable to resist, as pathetically needy. She could feel that need riot through him, taste it each time he dragged her mouth back to his with a ravenous hunger.

While her heart screamed at him to love her, just a little, her quivering body greedily devoured, fueling itself with whatever scraps he would give.

No room for pride, no time for tenderness.

When she sank toward him, limp as water, he rolled her ruthlessly onto her back and drove her on.

He couldn't breathe, didn't think, just battered himself into her. He had to fill her, to empty her, to claim her in the only way he knew she would accept. With a jerk of his head, he tossed the hair out of his eyes. It was vital that he see her, every flicker of shock and pleasure on her face, every tremble of her lips.

Love for her swamped him. All but destroyed him.

"Look at me." He grated the words out. "You look at me."

Her eyes opened, but remained blind with passion. He felt her body quake under his, saw those eyes glaze as her head fell back.

He was powerless to stop himself from following her recklessly over the edge. But he cursed her, then himself, as he fell.

It didn't seem possible to have been so completely aroused, and to feel so utterly empty. He'd never understood how vitally entwined the heart and the body were, until now. And now, staring at the ceiling, with Regan silent beside him, he understood it would never be possible to separate his again.

Not with her.

And he wanted only her.

She'd taken something from him that he'd struggled for years to build. His self-respect. How odd that he hadn't realized that, either, until this moment.

He wasn't sure he could forgive either of them for it.

She desperately wanted him to reach out to her, to fold her to him as he had in the past. It was miserable to be left like this, so cold, so alone, even as she was still quivering from him.

Yet how could she reach out for him, when she was the one who had taken the step, made the stand, and agreed to take him on his own terms? His own terms, she thought, closing her eyes against the lovely rosy glow of the lamp. Bad Rafe MacKade had returned, she thought bitterly, and taken it all.

"Well, we managed to have sex in a bed for a change." She sat up, kept her back to him. She could control her voice, but was certain her face would show him that she was shattered. "It's always firsts with us, isn't it, MacKade?"

"Yeah." He wanted to stroke that back, but it was so stiff and straight. "We'll have to try it with sheets sometime."

"Why not?" Her hands trembled as she slid off the bed, reached down for her underwear. "We could even throw in a couple of pillows, and a pretense of affection. Just for a change of pace."

His eyes sharpened, narrowed, as she snapped her bra into place. Hurt and fury bubbled together in a messy stew. Rising, he snatched his jeans, jammed his legs in them.

"I don't like pretenses much."

"Oh, that's right." She grabbed her shirt. Silk whipped through the air and onto her back. "Everything's up-front with you. No frills, no spills."

"What the hell's wrong with you? You got what you wanted."

"You don't know diddly about what I want." Terrified she might weep, she jerked on her slacks. "Apparently neither do I."

"You're the one who took off your clothes, darling." His voice was entirely too smooth. "You're the one putting them right back on so you can move right along."

"And you're the one who rolled off me the minute you were done, as if your twenty bucks was up." Rushing now, she jammed her feet into her shoes.

She might have had a chance if she'd been looking at him. A slim one. But he moved fast, and she was six inches off the ground, his hands like a vise on her, his eyes drilling holes in hers before she drew a second breath.

"Don't say that. I've never treated you that way. I've never thought that way."

"You're right." Oddly enough, it was the lash of his

temper that calmed her. Stopped her, she hoped, from being a perfect fool. "I'm sorry, Rafe. That was unfair and untrue."

Very slowly, he set her back on her feet. He realized his fingers were digging hard enough into her flesh to meet bone, and dropped his hands. "Maybe I moved too fast, but you caught me off guard."

"No." Yes, she felt very calm, she thought as she turned to pick up her blazer. Very calm, and very, very fragile. If he touched her again, she would crack like flawed glass. "I initiated things, and I agreed to your terms."

"My terms—"

"Are clear," she said, finishing for him. "And acceptable. I suppose the problem is that we're both volatile personalities under the right circumstances. Any circumstances, as far as you're concerned. And as for me, the past few days have been difficult. That doesn't mean I should take it out on you."

"Do you have to be reasonable, Regan?"

"No, but I'm going to be." Though her lips curved brightly, she couldn't move the smile into her eyes. "I don't know what we're fighting about, when we've found the perfect solution. A simple, physical relationship. It's perfect, because the rest of our common ground is narrow to nonexistent. So, I'll apologize again for picking a fight. I'm just a little tired and out of sorts."

She made herself rise on her toes and kiss him lightly. "If you'd like to come by tomorrow after work, I'll make it up to you."

"Yeah, maybe." Why the hell couldn't he read her eyes? He could always read her eyes if he looked hard enough. "I'll take you home."

"No, really." She had to will herself not to run to the door and escape. Instead, she picked up her purse. "I've got my car," she added. "And I really am tired. I could use an early night."

He just wanted to hold her, to fold her into his arms and keep her there. "Whatever you say. I'm supposed to meet my brothers at the tavern in a few hours, anyway."

"Good, then we'll try for tomorrow." She made it to the door without stumbling. He didn't offer a goodbye, and neither did she. Her coat was a bright red slash over the newel post, or she might have walked outside without it. She put in on, buttoned it carefully.

Outside, she got into her car, turned the key in the

ignition. She concentrated on backing down the lane as if her life depended on it. She took the turn toward town, drove a half mile.

Then she pulled over to the side of the road, carefully put the car in gear, turned the engine off. And cried like a baby.

Twenty minutes later, exhausted, she let her head fall back against the seat. It was freezing, but she didn't have the energy to turn the car on again and pump up the heater.

She was a competent woman, Regan thought. Everyone said so. She was bright, well-organized, moderately successful, and levelheaded.

So why, if she was indeed all of those fine, admirable things, had she managed to mess up her life so miserably?

Rafe MacKade was responsible, of course. She hadn't had a full day's easy running since he'd swaggered back into town. He was messy, arrogant, angry. Oh, so angry. And charming, she thought with a sigh, with all those unexpected sweet spots mixed with the rough.

She should never have fallen for him. She certainly

shouldn't have deluded herself that she could have an affair with him and stay objective.

He hadn't been completely objective, either, she remembered. He'd had feelings tangling him up, too. Before she'd ruined it. If she had been just a little more of what he needed, if she hadn't been so dead set on doing it all her way, he might have stayed tangled. Until he'd fallen in love.

Oh, that was wrong, she thought, and banged her fist against the steering wheel. That was her mother's kind of thinking. Make everything pretty, everything perfect for the man. Stroke his ego, cater to his whims. Play the game and win the prize.

Well, she wouldn't. She was appalled she'd even considered it. She would not squash her own needs, her own personality, her own ego, to lure a man into love.

But hadn't she just done that? She shuddered, but not from the cold. Hadn't she just done that, up in that bedroom?

At a loss, she braced her elbows on the wheel, her head in her hands. She wasn't sure of anything any longer. Except that she loved him. She loved him, and in her stubborn stance against luring him into love with her, she had blocked, perhaps even rejected his feelings. And humiliated herself in the bargain.

That, Regan concluded, made her an idiot.

So what if she had to make some changes in herself? Hadn't he, in his way, done the same?

He'd been hurt, she remembered. She had hurt him, infuriated him. Yet he had gone off to pound nails, instead of picking a fight. It was she who was the coward, who had been unwilling to trust, refusing to bend. He'd never tried to run her life, or her thoughts, or tried to change her. No, he'd given her room, he'd given her affection, and he'd given her the kind of passion a woman dreamed of.

But she'd held back anyway, foolishly, in a knee-jerk response rooted in her upbringing.

Why hadn't she thought of his needs, his pride? Wasn't it time she did so? She could be flexible, couldn't she? Compromise wasn't capitulation. It couldn't be too late to show him she was willing. She wouldn't let it be too late to...

The thought that came into her mind was so simple, and so ridiculous, she knew it had to be right. Without giving herself a moment to think it through, she revved up the car and hit the gas. In minutes, she was on Cassie's doorstep, banging.

"Regan." With Emma on her hip, Cassie dragged a hand through her tousled hair. "I was just—you've been crying." Alarm sprinted through her. "Joe—"

"No, no. I'm sorry. I didn't mean to scare you. I need help."

"What is it?" In a flash, Cassie had closed the door and locked it. "What's wrong?"

"What's nine-ball?"

"What—?" Baffled, Cassie set Emma down, gave her a little pat on the bottom to send her along. "What's nine-ball?"

"Yes. And where am I going to find a red leather miniskirt at this hour?"

Cassie thought for a moment, brushing a hand over the wet spot on her sweater that was courtesy of Emma's bath. "If that's what you want, we'll have to call Ed."

"Suck it in, sweetie."

"I am." Valiantly Regan gritted her teeth and held her breath as Ed tugged at the zipper of a skirt the size of a place mat.

"Trouble is, you've got a figure. I've got bones." Mouth clamped tight in determination, Ed hauled, and tugged. Then, with a wheeze of triumph, sat back on Cassie's bed. "She's on, but I wouldn't make any sudden moves."

"I don't think I can make *any* moves." Testing, Regan took a step. The skirt, already dangerously high, snuck up another fraction.

"You got a little height on me, too," Ed announced, and pulled out a cigarette. Her eyes sparkled with amusement as she let her rhinestone glasses fall to her chest. "If it was much shorter on you, Devin would have to arrest you."

"I can't see." Though she rose on her toes and turned carefully, Cassie's mirror offered nothing but a view from the waist up.

"You don't have to, honey. Take my word, he will."

"I got the kids settled," Cassie said as she walked in. She stopped short, her mouth forming a shocked circle. "Oh, my…"

"It's a hot little number," Ed agreed. When she'd worn it last time, at the Legion dance, eyes had popped loose. The way Regan was filling it out, Ed imagined they'd not only pop, but go flying across the room.

"Try those shoes with it now," she ordered. "I stuffed some tissue in the toes to bring 'em down to size."

Regan braced a hand on Cassie's dresser, stepped gingerly into the four-inch spikes. "I'll get a nosebleed in these."

"Honey, you'll cause nosebleeds." Ed gave a raspy laugh. "Now let's try some war paint." Happily she upended her enormous purse onto the bed.

"I'm not sure I can go through with this. It's a crazy idea."

"Don't go chicken on me now." Ed riffled her hand through a department-store array of cosmetics. "You want that man, don't you?"

"Yes, but—"

"Then sit down here on the bed and let me buff you up. This here red's a killer," she murmured fondly as she unscrewed a lipstick.

"I can't sit," Regan stated after a single attempt. "I'd damage an internal organ."

"Then stand." After making her choices, Ed rose and went to work. "Now, you said nine-ball, right?"

"Yeah."

In her forty-two years—forty-five, if God was

listening—she'd never seen a woman less likely to chalk a stick than Regan Bishop. "Ever play pool, honey?"

"Billiards." Regan uttered a silent prayer as Ed advanced with eyeliner. "With my father. Several times."

"Hell, honey, billiards ain't nothing. Why, nine-ball's the second-best thing you can do on a pool table." She cackled when Cassie flushed scarlet. "Now listen up while I explain how it works."

Balls smacked and clattered when Rafe shot his cue. The five ball thumped satisfactorily into the corner pocket.

"Luck," Jared said, and lazily chalked his cue.

Rafe only snorted. "Six off the nine and in the side." He made his shot, lined up the next.

"Never could beat Rafe at nine-ball." More interested in the little redhead at the bar than the game, Shane leaned on the juke. She was all alone, and looked as cuddly as a new down pillow. "Seen her around before, Dev?"

Devin glanced up, over. "Holloway's niece, from up

on Mountain View. She's got a boyfriend the size of a semi who'll break you in half if you breathe on her."

It was all the challenge Shane needed. He sauntered over, leaned on the bar and turned on the charm.

Devin gave a resigned smile. If the boyfriend came in, Devin would have to use his badge. And that would blow his night.

"My game." Rafe held out his hand for the ten dollars Jared owed him. "You're up, Dev."

"I need a beer."

"Jared's buying." Rafe grinned at his older brother. "Right, bro?"

"I bought last round."

"You lost the last game."

"So be a gracious winner. His tab," Jared told the bartender, and held up three fingers.

"Hey, what about me?"

Jared flicked a glance at Shane. The redhead was clutching his arm like a fast-growing vine. "You're driving, kid."

"Flip for it."

Obligingly, Jared took a coin from his pocket. "Call it."

"Heads."

He flipped the coin, caught it neatly. "Tails. You're driving."

With a philosophical shrug, Shane turned back to the redhead.

"Does he have to hit on everything in a skirt?" Rafe muttered while Devin racked the balls.

"Yep. Somebody had to take up where you left off." Devin stepped back, chose his cue. "And since you're spoken for…"

"Nobody said I was spoken for." Rafe gave the curvy redhead a long look, felt nothing more than a low-level tug of basic appreciation. And thought of Regan, just thought of her and his heart shattered. "We've got an understanding." He bit the words off, but still tasted bitterness. "Nothing serious."

"He's hooked." Jared grinned and lifted his beer. "And his heart looks so pretty, right there on his sleeve."

No way he was going to take the bait, Rafe thought. It was bad enough having your heart broken without having your family watch you fumble with the pieces. "You want to eat this cue?" Rafe executed his break, smugly pleased when two balls rolled into pockets.

"She came into the house today," Devin said conversationally, "and that hook in his mouth dragged him right down the stairs like a trout on a fly. I think there were stars in his eyes, too." Devin met Rafe's steely look equably. "Yep, I'm sure of it."

"Pretty soon he's going to start shaving regular and wearing clean shirts." Jared shook his head, as if in mourning. "Then we'll know we've lost him."

"Then it'll be antique shows and ballets." Devin heaved a heavy sigh. "Poetry readings."

Because that hit entirely too close to home, Rafe jerked the cue and missed his shot. He wasn't going to think of her. Damn it, he wasn't going to give Regan or the hole in his gut a single thought. "Keep it up and I'll take both of you on."

"Well, I'm shaking." After lining up his shot, Devin leaned over the table. He made his ball cleanly. As he circled the table, he sniffed at Rafe. "That cologne, lover-boy?"

"I'm not wearing any damn—" Rafe hissed out a breath. "You're just jealous 'cause you're sleeping alone on some cot outside a cell every night."

"You got me there."

Enjoying himself, Jared plugged coins into the jukebox. "What time do you have to be home, Rafe? We wouldn't want you getting conked with a rolling pin for missing curfew."

"How long have you been a practicing ass?" It was some small satisfaction to note that Duff was shooting them uneasy glances. A man didn't like to lose his touch. "What's the fine for breaking up a couple of chairs?"

Nostalgia swam sweetly along with the beer in Devin's bloodstream. Unless he counted breaking his brothers up, and you could hardly count that, he hadn't been in a decent fight in years.

"Can't let you do it," he said, with mildly drunk regret. "I carry a badge."

"Take it off." Rafe grinned. "And let's beat hell out of Shane. For old times' sake."

Jared tapped his fingers on the juke in time to the music. He eyed their youngest brother, who was definitely making progress with the redhead. That alone was reason enough to punch him a few times.

"I've got enough on me to post bond," Jared told them. "And a little extra to bribe the sheriff, if we have to."

Devin sighed, straightened from the table. With brotherly affection, he studied the unsuspecting Shane. "Hell, he's going to get his butt whipped before the night's over, anyway, if he keeps playing with that girl. We might as well do it first."

"We'll be more humane," Jared agreed.

The bartender watched them move together, recognized, with despair, the look in each eye. "Not in here. Come on now, Devin, you're the law."

"Just doing my brotherly duty."

"What's the idea?" Scenting trouble, Shane danced back from the bar. He scanned his brothers, shifted as they moved to flank him. "Three against one?" His mouth curved in a wide, reckless grin as other customers moved to safety. "Come on, then."

He crouched, braced, then made the mistake of glancing over as the door opened. His mouth had already fallen open in surprise when Rafe caught him low and sent them both crashing into a table.

"You make it too easy." Laughing, Rafe turned and caught him in a cheerful headlock. Then he went numb, right down to his toes.

The skirt barely made it past the legal limit. It wasn't

tight. It went beyond tight as it squeezed possessively over curvy hips in an eye-popping fire-engine red. The legs went on. And on. Rafe's dazzled gape followed them down to the razor-sharp skyscraper heels in that same bold color.

When he managed to lift his gaze, he saw that the skinny black top was as snug as the skirt, and dipped down low over firm, unfettered breasts. It took him a full ten seconds to get to her face.

Her mouth was red and wet and curved. Beside it, the little mole was a bold exclamation of sex. Her hair was tousled, and her eyes were shadowed and heavy. She looked like a woman who'd just climbed out of bed, and was willing to climb right back in.

"Holy hell." It was Shane's strained muttering that jolted him out of shock. "Is that Regan in there? She is *hot*."

Rafe didn't have the strength to put much behind the punch. When he gained his feet and moved to the door, his head was still buzzing, as if he'd been the one to take the blow.

"What are you doing?"

She moved a shoulder, causing the excuse for a

blouse to follow her stretch. "I thought I'd play a little nine-ball."

There was something stuck in his throat. "Nine-ball?"

"Yeah." She sauntered over to the bar, leaned an elbow on it. "Going to buy me a beer, MacKade?"

Chapter 12

If he kept staring at her, she was going to lose it, Regan thought. She was already so nervous that if her clothes hadn't been girdled on, she'd have jumped out of them.

Because she'd wanted to make an entrance, she'd left her coat in the car. Only the heat of possible humiliation kept her teeth from chattering.

Her feet were killing her.

When Rafe didn't answer, she scanned the room and tried not to swallow audibly at the stares. Gathering courage, she flashed a smile at the bartender. Even the weary-eyed Duff was goggling at her.

"I'll have what he's having." When she had the beer in her hand, she turned back. No one had moved a muscle. It was either run or play it out, Regan told herself, taking a quick swallow of beer.

She hated beer.

"Are you going to rack them, MacKade, or am I?"

"I'll rack them," Jared interjected helpfully. His hands were still a little sweaty, but he'd gotten over the worst of the shock. Rafe's face was almost as much of a pleasure to watch as the sway of Regan's hips, as she sauntered over to study the arsenal of cues.

Rafe heard the clatter of balls, and blinked. "You said you wanted an early night."

"Changed my mind." Her voice was breathy from necessity, rather than design. The leather and Spandex were cutting off her air supply. "I had all this…energy all of a sudden." She walked slowly to the table, resisting the urge to tug at the hem of the skirt. "Who wants to play?"

Half a dozen men moved with scraping chairs and clattering boots. Rafe's snarl was the low, vicious sound of a wild dog guarding his bone. Half a dozen men decided they weren't in the mood for pool after all.

"This is a joke, right?"

Regan took the cue Devin offered, smiled and stroked her fingertips from the tip down the shaft. Someone moaned. "I felt like some action, that's all."

With her confidence building, she passed the bottle of beer to Jared. This, at least, she thought, she knew how to do. Planting her feet, bending one knee for balance, she leaned over the table. Leather strained.

Rafe's elbow plowed into Shane's gut. "Keep looking where you're looking, and you'll be blind for a week."

"Jeez, Rafe." Shane tucked his hands in his pockets and prepared to watch the show. "Where's a guy supposed to look?"

She broke cleanly, even managed to sink a ball. With the rules of the game Ed had drilled into her flipping through her head, she circled the table. She had to stop, smile, as Devin was still rooted in her path.

"You're blocking the table, Sheriff."

"Oh. Yeah, right. Sorry." When she draped herself over the felt this time, his eyes met Jared's. They grinned at each other like two kids over a shiny new bike.

She managed to sink one more. That made her cocky enough to try a complicated shot that required a little English. Her hips wiggled as she set her position. From behind her, Jared stuck a hand under his shirt and mimed a thumping heart.

"You think what you're thinking again, and I'll rip your lungs out," Rafe muttered.

As the ball missed the pocket by a good six inches, Regan pouted with that red-slicked mouth. "Oops." She straightened, batted thickly mascaraed eyes at Rafe. "Your turn." She put her weight on one foot and ran a hand down his shirtfront. "Want me to...chalk your cue?"

The room exploded with whoops and whistles. Some brave soul made a suggestion that had Rafe's lips peeling back in a growl. "That does it."

He grabbed her cue, tossed it at Devin, then clamped a hand over hers to drag her toward the door.

"But we haven't finished the game," she protested, forced to scramble on the skinny heels to keep up with him.

He yanked his jacket from the hook by the door and bundled it around her. "Put this on before I have to kill somebody." She was still struggling with it when he shoved her through the door.

Devin let out a long, appreciative sigh. "He's a dead man."

"Yeah." Shane rubbed a hand over his stomach. "Did you ever notice her—"

In Rafe's stead, Jared rapped him with a cue.

"I have my car," Regan began, while Rafe towed her along.

He dragged open the door of his own. "Get in. Now."

"I could follow you."

"Now."

"All right." It wasn't a simple operation to get into his car. Snug red leather rode higher as she tried for graceful and dignified as she lowered herself into the seat. Rafe ground his teeth audibly. "Where are we going?"

"I'm taking you home." He slammed her door, stormed around the hood, then slammed his own hard enough to rock the car. "And if you're smart, you won't talk to me."

She was smart. When his brakes squealed at the base of her steps, she stayed where she was. There was no possible way she could maneuver herself out of the tiny sports car without help.

He gave it to her, though no one would have called the hard yank a gentlemanly gesture. "Keys," he snapped, then snatched them out of her hand and unlocked the door himself.

Miffed, she strode in ahead of him. "I assume you're coming in, so——"

She was rapped back against the door, his mouth hotly devouring hers. The heels put them head-to-head, heat to heat, with a pressure that fried his already overheated brain. Both his mouth and his hands were hard, possessive. He could only think of branding her his.

His breath was ragged when he jerked back. He'd be damned if she'd work him this way again, make him a victim of his own needs.

He tugged his jacket off her shoulders, tossed it aside. "Get out of those clothes."

Something in her sank. With her lashes lowered, she reached around for the zipper of the skirt.

"No, I didn't mean— God." If she peeled herself out of that leather in front of him, he was lost. It was the confusion in her eyes that had him leveling his voice.

"I meant I'd appreciate it if you changed into something else. Please."

"I thought you—"

"I know what you thought." He was dying here. "Just change, so I can talk to you."

"All right."

He knew it was a mistake to watch her walk toward the bedroom. But he was only human.

Inside, Regan stepped out of the ankle-breaking shoes, stripped off the red leather. It was good to breathe again. She wanted to be amused, at both of them, but she felt so incredibly stupid. She'd made a spectacle of herself, thrown aside every scrap of dignity. For nothing.

No, she thought as she fastened on pleated trousers. For him. She'd done it for him, and he didn't even have the sense to appreciate it.

When she came back in, face washed, her hair brushed back into place, an ivory sweater tucked neatly into the waistband of black slacks, he was pacing.

"I want to know what you were thinking of," he said without preamble. "Just what you were thinking of, walking into a bar dressed like that?"

"It was your idea," she tossed back, but he was too busy clenching his jaw and muttering to himself to listen.

"Five more minutes in there, and we'd have had a riot. I'd have started it myself. I've seen you naked, and I'm not sure I knew you were built like that. Now everybody in town's going to know."

"You said you wanted—"

"I don't give a damn what they say about me, but nobody's going to talk behind their hands about you. Where the hell did you get that skirt?" he exploded. "Tarts R Us?"

"Well, really…"

"Yeah, really. And leaning over the pool table that way, so everyone was looking at your—"

Her eyes narrowed to slits. "Watch it, MacKade."

"Now I'm going to have to go bash all of my brothers' brains in for what they were thinking."

"You like bashing their brains in," she retorted.

"That's beside the point."

"I'll give you a point."

She picked up her favorite Milton vase and tossed it to the floor. Rather than smashing satisfactorily, it bounced and rolled on the dainty floral rug. But the gesture shut him up.

"I humiliated myself for you. It nearly took a crowbar to get me into that ridiculous skirt, and I think I bruised my intestines. I'll probably never get all this makeup out of my pores, my arches are screaming, and I have not an ounce of dignity left. I hope you're satisfied."

"I—"

"Shut up. This time you just *shut up.* You wanted me to be that way, so I tried. I was willing to be what you wanted, and now all you can do is stand there and criticize and worry about gossip. Well, go to hell!"

She plopped down in a chair, because her feet were cramping painfully.

He waited until he was sure she'd run down, watched her sniffle and rub her bare feet. "You did that for me?"

"No, I did it because I like teetering on four-inch heels and going around half-naked in the middle of winter. I live for it," she said nastily.

"You did it to get to me."

The bout of temper had drained her. She sat back, closed her eyes. "I did it because I'm crazy about you.

Just like you said I'd be. Now go away and leave me alone. You'll have to wait till tomorrow to beat your chest and drag me off by the hair. I'm too tired."

He studied her a moment, then walked to the door and shut it quietly behind him.

She didn't bother to get up, or even to move. She didn't feel like crying. If she'd been ridiculous, she would weather it. She'd given him everything now, and there was no taking it back. Why should she bother? She'd never stop loving him.

She heard the door open again, and kept her eyes closed. "I really am tired, Rafe. Can't you gloat to-morrow?"

Something fell into her lap. Regan blinked her eyes open and stared at the bouquet of lilacs.

"They're not real," he told her. "You can't get them in February. I've had them in the trunk of my car for a few days, so they're cold."

"They're lovely." Slowly she ran her fingers over the chilly silk blooms. "A few days," she murmured, and looked up again.

"Yeah, so?" He scowled, jammed his hands in his pockets, shifted. "Man." He thought facing a noose would be easier than what he was about to do. It certainly couldn't burn his throat any less.

He got down on his knees.

"What are you doing?"

"Just keep quiet," he warned her. "And if you laugh, you pay." Mortified, he swore under his breath, dragged a hand through his hair. And bit the bullet.

"'When I arose and saw the dawn, I sighed for thee.'"

"Rafe..."

"Don't interrupt me." Miserably embarrassed, he glared at her. "Now I have to start over."

"But you don't have to—"

"Regan."

She drew in a breath, wondered if there was another woman in the world who had ever had Shelley quoted to her with eyes that threatened murder. "Sorry. You were saying?"

He shifted his weight. "Okay. 'When I arose and saw the dawn, I sighed for thee; When the light rode high, and the dew was gone, and...' Oh, hell." He raked his fingers through his hair and tried to concentrate. "I got it. 'And noon lay heavy on flower and tree, And the weary Day turned to her rest, lingering like an unloved guest, I sighed for thee.'"

His breath came out on a huff of tremendous relief. "That's all I've got. It took me more than a week to memorize it. If you mention this to anyone—"

"I wouldn't dream of it." Incredibly moved, she laid a hand on his cheek. "That was very sweet of you."

"It kind of fits the way I feel about you." And now that it was over—thank God—it hadn't been as bad as he'd feared. "I think about you, Regan, all day. Every day. So if you want poetry—"

"No." With a quick shake of her head, she reached out and laid her cheek on his shoulder. "No, I don't need poetry, Rafe."

"I haven't bothered to give you much romance." And he knew now, by the way her eyes had gone soft and dreamy, that he should have. "Now it's fake flowers and somebody else's words."

She had to cry now, but they were lovely tears, soothing ones. "I love the flowers, and I loved the words. But I don't need them. I don't want you to change for me, Rafe. There's nothing about you I'd want to change. I said I'd take you as you are and I mean it."

"I like you the way you are, Regan, all neat and tidy. Not that I didn't appreciate the way you filled out that leather."

"I'm sure I could borrow it from Ed again."

"Ed?" He rolled his eyes and chuckled weakly. "No wonder it fit you like skin." Then he felt the warm drops on his neck. "Oh, don't do that, baby. Please don't."

"I'm not really crying. I'm just touched that you'd memorize Shelley for me. That you'd care enough." She gave him a hard squeeze before leaning back. "I guess we both won the bet, or lost it, depending on your viewpoint." She dried off her cheeks with the back of her hand. "Of course, you didn't lose yours in public."

"If you think you can talk me into giving that little recital down at the tavern, you really are crazy. I'd never get out alive."

She drew in a deep breath. "I think we should both stick with who and what we are. I do like who and what you are, Rafe. And I need you more than you think. I needed you when Joe came into the shop and frightened me. I just didn't want you to know it. I was afraid to let you know how much I count on you."

He picked up her hand, kissed it, and felt dozens of wounds heal. "You didn't have to be."

"I figured that out for myself. I like figuring things out for myself."

"Tell me about it." He smiled and no longer felt foolish being on his knees. "I like the way you figure things out for yourself. The way you handle yourself, Regan. Even when it ticks me off, I like your style."

"I like yours, too." She leaned forward and kissed him lightly. "I'm going to get something to put these in."

He reached behind him and picked up the vase she'd thrown. "How about this?"

"That'll be fine." She took it from him and rose to arrange the silk bouquet on the table. "I can't believe I actually threw it."

"It's been an eventful evening. So far."

She glanced back, smiled. "It certainly has. Would you like to stay, and see what happens next?"

"There we are, on the same wavelength again. You know, Regan, I think we've got more common ground than either one of us realized. You shoot decent pool, I like antiques." He stood, moving restlessly, picked up a china cat in suddenly nerveless fingers, then set it down again. "So, you want to get married?"

She tucked a sprig of lilacs into place. "Hmm... You asked me that before, as I remember. And never took me up on it, because I won't watch baseball."

"I mean it."

She twirled to face him, and her limp hand knocked against the table. "Excuse me?"

"Look, we haven't known each other very long." He stepped toward her, stopped cold. She was staring at him as though he'd lost his mind. He was certain he had. "But we've got something going here. I know we said it was just going to be sex, and we've just finished deciding we really like each other."

"Rafe, I can't—"

"If you'd just let me fumble through this." His tone went from quiet to testy in an instant. "I know how you are with having to weigh your options and think things through. But the least you can do is look at this from my perspective for one damn minute. It's not just sex for me, and it never was. I'm in love with you."

She stared into those sharp, angry eyes, heard the treasured phrase delivered in a furious snarl. And felt her heart swell like a rose blooming in her chest. "You're in love with me," she repeated.

It had always been easy to say the words when it didn't count—when they were just words, and not these tiny, razor-edged little pellets in his throat. "I'm in love with you," he said again. "It probably happened five minutes after I met you, maybe five minutes before. I don't know. It's never happened to me before."

"Me, either," she murmured.

He didn't hear her, didn't hear anything but the roaring in his head. "No one's ever needed me. I've never wanted anyone to need me. It gets in the way. But I want that from you. I have to ask that from you." He paused, fought to steady himself. "I don't like asking."

"I know. You don't have to." She walked to him, framed his face in her hands. "Rafe, you don't have to ask."

"If you'd give me a chance—" he gripped her wrists "—I could make it work. We could make it work. Come on, Regan, take a risk. Live dangerously."

"Yes."

His grip on her wrists went lax. "Yes, what?"

"Why do we have such a hard time hearing each

other?" she asked. "Listen up," she ordered, and kissed him firmly. "Yes, I'll marry you."

"Just like that? You're not going to think about it?"

"Nope."

"Good. Great." A little dazed, he stepped back. "We could, ah, t-take care of…it. Take care of it tomorrow. The license. Whatever. You want a ring…or something?"

"Yes, I do. Rafe, you're stuttering."

"No, I'm not." He stepped back when she stepped forward. "I just didn't expect you to take the jump so quick."

"If you're trying to change your mind, forget it. Was it the skirt?"

His eyes went blank and baffled. "What skirt?"

No answer could have pleased her more. "I think you should tell me you love me again." Before he could evade her, she wrapped her arms around his neck, linked her fingers. "I think you should get used to saying it."

"I do love you."

"And you were in love with me that first night, when we were alone, in the house on the hill?"

"I guess I was."

"I didn't know, didn't have a clue. I wonder if the house did. I remember how quiet it got that night— how settled it all seemed. Would you like to go back there, tonight?"

"Yes." He rested his brow on hers. "I would."

"There's something I should tell you first, Rafe. Something I think we should clear up between us."

"Regan, if you're going to slap down more rules and parameters—"

"I think I should tell you," she said interrupting him, "that as attracted as I was to you, as aroused as I was by you, I could have slept with you without loving you."

"I know." He refused to be hurt by it. "It's okay."

"I could have done that because you're the most incredibly attractive man I've ever met, all the way through. But there's no way I would have squeezed myself into that ridiculous outfit tonight unless I'd been wildly, stupidly and completely in love with you." Her eyes shimmered and smiled. "Is that okay?"

"Say it again." He took her face in his hands. "Look at me straight-on and say it again."

"I love you. I'm so very much in love with you,

Rafe. There's nothing I want more than to go on loving you, and needing you for the rest of my life."

The thrill of it sprinted through him, then settled, warm and easy. "You could get used to saying it, too."

"I'm a very quick study. I love you," she murmured against his mouth, then poured the words into the kiss.

"It's going to get complicated." He gathered her close and held her. Just held her. "Life's going to be messy."

"I hope so." Eyes closed, she pressed her cheek against his. "Oh, I hope so. Why was I so scared?" she whispered. "Why was I so afraid to let you know?"

"Probably for the same reason I was." He tilted her head back. "It happened so fast, and it matters so much. And it always will."

"It always will," she agreed.

Later, when they were curled together in the deep feather bed, she laid her hand on his heart and smiled.

"I'm awfully glad you came back to town, MacKade. Welcome home."

The house was quiet around them, and slept as they slept.

* * * * *

The World of Mills & Boon®

There's a Mills & Boon® series that's perfect for you. We publish ten series and, with new titles every month, you never have to wait long for your favourite to come along.

Blaze®

Scorching hot, sexy reads
4 new stories every month

By Request

Relive the romance with the best of the best
9 new stories every month

Cherish™

Romance to melt the heart every time
12 new stories every month

Desire™

Passionate and dramatic love stories
8 new stories every month

Have Your Say

You've just finished your book.
So what did you think?

We'd love to hear your thoughts on our 'Have your say' online panel
www.millsandboon.co.uk/haveyoursay

- 🌹 Easy to use
- 🌹 Short questionnaire
- 🌹 Chance to win Mills & Boon® goodies

Visit us
Online

Tell us what you thought of this book now at
www.millsandboon.co.uk/haveyoursay

YOUR_SAY